ACTION IN THE SPUR SALOON

Kilkenny strode into the room. "Where's Polti?" he demanded.

"You won't get any answers here, mister," the seated man taunted. "When Polti wants you, he'll get you."

Half-turning his head, Kilkenny caught a glimpse of an upraised bottle, poised for throwing. His pistol leaped to his hand and the gun roared, bottle and fragments scattering.

Kilkenny stepped in quickly and caught the bottle-thrower by the shirt front, jerking him into the punch he threw into his belly. He shoved him away, then uppercut hard to the face. The bottle-thrower hit the floor and rolled over.

Spinning quickly, Kilkenny kicked the outstretched legs of the seated man. He came off the chair and hit the floor on his rump with a thud.

Kilkenny stepped in and as the man gathered himself to rise, he kicked him in the face.

"I came in here," he said gently, "for a little polite conversation, but if you like it this way, you can have it."

LOUIS L'AMOUR
THE RIDER
OF LOST CREEK

BANTAM BOOKS
TORONTO · NEW YORK · LONDON

THE RIDER OF LOST CREEK
A Bantam Book / August 1976
2nd printing . September 1976   3rd printing ... October 1976
4th printing .... May 1977
5th printing
6th printing

ISBN 0-553-11119-1

Published simultaneously in the United States and Canada

Bantam Books are published by Bantam Books, Inc. Its trade-
mark, consisting of the words "Bantam Books" and the por-
trayal of a bantam, is registered in the United States Patent
Office and in other countries. Marca Registrada. Bantam
Books, Inc., 666 Fifth Avenue, New York, New York 10019.

PRINTED IN THE UNITED STATES OF AMERICA

CHAPTER I

A lone cowhand riding a hard-pressed horse stepped down from the saddle and whipped the dust from his hat by a few stiff blows against his chaps. He stood for an instant looking up and down the street, crowded with buckboards, saddle-horses and men. It was ten o'clock in the morning but Dodge was a twenty-four-hour town with thirty thousand head of cattle held on the grass outside of town, and more coming in every day.

Pushing his way through the bat-wing doors, he crossed the almost empty room to the bar. "Rye," he said, and glanced quickly around the room.

Only two men stood at the bar at this hour, a burly cattle-buyer and a drummer, the latter still only half awake and nursing a hangover from the night before.

Several other men played cards at the scattered tables, all within range of his voice.

"Never would've believed it," the cowhand said, "but they're stringin' wire on the plains of Texas!"

"Ain't practical," the cattle-buyer said dogmatically. "That there's a free range country and it should stay thataway. They'll never stand for it, anyway."

"Don't make no difference," the cowhand insisted. "They're doin' it." He glanced around the room again and his tone lowered. "Have you seen Kilkenny?"

There was a sudden stillness in the room. The cattle-buyer glanced uneasily at the bartender, who was suddenly very busy mopping the bar. For a long moment nobody spoke.

A cattleman at the nearest poker table picked up his cards, glanced at them, folded them into a neat packet

1

and placed them on the table. "No, I haven't seen him, and I'm not likely to . . . Nor are you. He's a man who prefers to be left alone, and if you know anything about Kilkenny you know he's a good man to leave alone."

"I've been sent to find him," the puncher said stubbornly, "an' I'm to stay at it until I do."

A man had moved to the bar beside him. He was a square-shouldered young man with a look about him the cowhand did not like. Moreover, he knew the man by sight, as did a good many Texas men. Wes Hardin was a veteran of the Sutton-Taylor feud and one of the most feared men in Texas. When men talked of guns and gunfighters, they spoke of him in the same breath with Bill Hickok, Royal Barnes and the Brockman twins.

"What do you want with Kilkenny?" Hardin asked.

"Looks like a range war shapin' up in the Live Oak country," the puncher told them. "They're shapin' up for a shootin' war, sure enough."

"Don't look for Kilkenny, then," the cattle-buyer advised. "He's a man who minds his own affairs. He wouldn't be a paid warrior for any man. If you're looking for a fighting man for a range war, you'd better hunt somebody else."

"You won't have to look far, either," the bartender commented grimly. "If there's one gunman in this town, there's fifty . . . and fifty more nearly as good."

"This is different," the puncher replied. "My boss is an old friend of his."

"Somebody said he was riding with King Fisher's outfit," a gambler suggested.

"Don't you believe it!" the cattle-buyer said. "He never rode with any outfit except as a cowhand. He plays a lone hand, keeps pretty much to himself. Last I heard he was buffalo huntin' down near Adobe Walls with Billy Dixon and Bat Masterson."

The bartender stopped mopping the bar and refilled the cowboy's glass. "On the house," he said quietly. "You say you're bringing word from an old friend of Kilkenny's? Give us a name. There might be somebody here would pass the word along . . . and it's the only way you'll find him."

"Mort Davis," the cowhand tasted the rye. "Just tell him Mort Davis is in trouble. Kilkenny won't need more than that, for he's said to stick by his friends."

"That's what they say," the cattle-buyer commented, "and I do recall some story about Mort Davis."

"Hell," Hardin replied, "everybody knows that story! Kilkenny had a shoot-out with the three Weber boys and wiped them out, then some of their outfit chased him down . . . he was badly wounded . . . and Mort Davis had taken him in and was caring for him when that outfit came in and tried to take him away from Mort to lynch him.

"Mort Davis told them where they could go, and stood them off with a Spencer fifty-six until they decided they could have more fun somewhere else with less trouble. You don't forget a man like that . . . and Mort was a complete stranger to Kilkenny until he rode in there, half-dead."

"The word was out that Royal Barnes was huntin' Kilkenny," somebody commented. "He was kin to the Webers, you know. Half-brother, I think."

"Wouldn't that be something! Royal Barnes and Kilkenny! Two of the fastest gunmen in the west!"

"The difference is," the cattle-buyer replied, "that Barnes parades it. Kilkenny never did. He just happened to come out ahead in several gun battles with men who weren't smart enough to know better. He never looked for the name, and never wanted it."

"What's he look like?" somebody asked. "I never seen him."

"Nobody agrees," the cattle-buyer commented. "I've heard two dozen descriptions of the man, and every one of them different. He never seems to make himself known until the shooting starts and then he takes out right after.

"All they seem to agree on is that he's tall, minds his own affairs, and he's not inclined to talk very much. I also hear he's a top hand in any outfit, a damn good straight-up bronc rider and a good hand with a rope.

"He's done some freighting, rode shotgun on a stage a few times, and they say that during the war between the states he was a dispatch rider for the Union. He scouted for the army in some of the Indian wars, and he's Irish. Beyond that I don't think anybody knows very much."

"There's a whole colony of Irish down there in the Live Oak country," the gambler commented. "Brought in there in the 1840s, I think."

"There's French, Germans and Swiss, too," Hardin added, "several colonies around San Antone and New Braunfels."

"Where can a man get a bite to eat?" the cowhand asked.

"There's several restaurants, but if you can do with beef an' eggs, just set down over yonder and we can fix you up. They're fixin' breakfast for the boss right now," the bartender added, "and I'll just have them put on something extry."

When the bartender saw the puncher sit down at a table by himself, he filled a cup with coffee and walked over. "This is a good place to hear the news," he said quietly. "If I was you I'd just take my time eatin' and talk to the boss awhile and just keep your eyes open. This here is as good place as any to spread the word."

He added: "The way I figure it, you won't see Kilkenny, but if he hears Mort Davis is in trouble, he'll just come riding, and I have an idea you'll be able to go back home with a clear mind."

"Thanks," the cowhand gulped the coffee, glancing around the room as he did so. A dozen men had drifted in by ones and twos, and conversation flowered in the room. Here and there he could hear a word or two, and most of the talk was of cattle, horses and men, of trail drives and range conditions and the going price for beef on the hoof. All was familiar, even the brass spittoons and the brass rail along the bar.

Even many of the faces were faces he knew from

Texas, or from trail drives to Abilene, Newton or Ellsworth, and if not the faces, the style of the men themselves. They came in all sizes and shapes, but there was a common resemblance. All were hard, tough men living out a dangerous game—driving cattle up a thousand miles of trail from Texas.

Through the fog of conversation he heard casual talk of Kilkenny. The mystery of the man fascinated them, and yet from all Mort had said, and from what the cattle-buyer had added, Kilkenny sought no mystery and no reputation, and simply went his own way.

Kilkenny, someone said, was faster than Hickok or Hardin, and had the nerve of Ben Thompson. One man had been in Missouri where two would-be bad men had cornered Kilkenny. Both died before they could fire a shot.

Some of the stories, the cowhand was sure, were simply fiction, or stories taken from what was known of some other gunfighter, somewhere.

"This bob-wire," somebody said, "won't last in Texas. It's free range and so it will always be. God made that grass for cows just like he did for buffalo, and nobody can rightfully fence it in. When the buffalo ran, it was free grass, and so it will always be."

"I don't know," another said doubtfully. "A man likes to know his own cattle, and to have his own range. There were millions of buffalo, but they never grazed the same ground two days in succession. They just kept moving along, north to south. If you get to holding cattle on the range they'll eat up all that grass in no time. I can understand the thinking of those who want fenced range, but personally, I'm against it."

"What about this range war?"

"Hell, it's no secret! I've heard the Brockman twins are in it, and half a dozen others just as mean. And who's to stop them?"

"What about the Rangers?"

"They're too busy with the Kiowas and the Comanches, or bandits raids from south of the border. Anyway, most of those Rangers would have friends on one side or the other."

"It's the hoe-men you've got to consider. Farmers comin' out from back east who know nothin' about range stock, and care less. They'll fence plow-land and pasture, and they'll fight to keep the cattle out. I think the day of free grass is finished!"

"Did you ever foller a trail herd?" a cowboy scoffed. "This here is *range* country, an' it ain't fit for farmin'. If they ever plow that land, the wind will blow it the hell into Mexico!"

The cowhand ran his fingers along his unshaven jaw. Now if there was time, a bath and a shave would be right nice, and maybe a look at the girls down on the Line before he started the long ride back to Texas.

Of course, it would not be the lonely ride it would have been a few years back, for there were trail herds scattered along the route all the way. He'd be able to ride the grub-line from chuck wagon to chuck wagon.

A big, broad-shouldered man with graying hair hair walked over and sat down with him, tucking a napkin into his collar. "You the rider from Texas? I'm John Hohner." He gestured about him. "I operate this place." Then he added, "I was born down in Fredericksburg."

"I am huntin' Lance Kilkenny," the cowhand said.

"He's a good man. You ride for Mort Davis? I knew Mort, some years back. Tall man . . . blond?"

"He's no such thing," the cowhand said. "He's a medium short man with dark hair and a broken nose. He's part Irish and part German and a mite English, and he's a darn good cattleman."

"All right," Hohner agreed, "but I can't trust any drifter who comes in here looking for Kilkenny. The man has enemies . . ."

"I thought they were mostly dead," the cowhand said.

"As a matter of fact, the only dead ones are those who tried to prove something. He's a peaceful man when left alone, and I respect that. He's never put himself forward—others have done it for him; and it's simply that in a country where most disagreements are settled with guns, he has come out ahead. He's good.

There's no question of that. I've seen him in action twice, and I would never have believed the man lived who could get into action so fast or shoot so straight.

"I don't know where he is, but I do know how to get word to him. My best guess would be that he should know within the week that Mort Davis is in trouble. Knowing the man, my bet would be that within the hour—once he knows Mort's in trouble—Kilkenny will be riding south.

"He'll travel alone, I expect, and he'll chose his own way, and he's not likely to go down the Chisholm Trail . . . or any well-traveled route."

"What about water?"

"He'll find water. He can find water where a coyote would die for lack of it, and he leaves no more trail than a ghost . . . I have that from a Delaware who tried to find him for the Army, when he was needed."

"Just so's he comes. I'm no hand with a six-shooter more'n the average, an' that's a tough outfit we're facin'. You tell him to ride careful, for they'll be out to kill any man they don't know on the idea that if he isn't one of theirs he must naturally be an enemy. If I get back to the ranch with my hair, I'll need all the luck in the world."

"All right," Hohner replied. "If you need anything for the trail, just tell Ray at the bar. He'll see that you have it."

Hohner paused a moment and then said, more quietly, "Son? If I were you I'd put all those ideas about a girl and a few drinks out of my mind. If you want to live to see Texas, you'll leave within the hour."

"Huh? Are you crazy? I just got in, an' the boss said—"

"I don't care what he said. Your boss isn't in Dodge. He's in Texas. By now there isn't a man on the street who doesn't know there's a rider in town from Texas hunting Kilkenny. And among those men who know are three of Webb Steele's riders who've been up here recruiting gun-hands.

"Now I've got a horse outside the back door. That horse is a fast black with a lot of guts and its wearing an HR brand. That horse now wears your bridle, saddle and rifle, and if you're half as smart as I think you are you'll ride north out of town to where Jake Breslin is holding the HR herd. You'll stay there until about sundown. And then you'll ride east about three or four miles and then cut south for Texas, avoiding any cattle herds you find.

"I'd ride all night, if I were you. There's another HR herd coming up the trail and you should run into it about three days south of here. Swap horses there and keep going."

The cowhand stared glumly at his food. "Hell!" he said. "And I was all ready for—"

"There's other days and other times. As well as other girls . . . if you live."

Hohner paused. "By now at least one of those Steele riders is watching your horse, which is in the livery stable. I had it put there within ten minutes after you walked into this place. They will have at least one man watching the trail south, and at least one more hunting you here in town."

"I had no idea," the cowhand muttered. "I didn't figure there'd be any of that outfit in town."

"There is," Hohner said quietly, "and they have hired at least two Colorado renegades already. The word is that Steele intends to ride roughshod over Chet Lord as well as Mort Davis and a few others. He's hired some real rough lads from over on Macho Creek, and he's ready."

"Gimme another cup of coffee and I'll hit the saddle," the cowhand said. He was a tough, barrel-chested man, his jaws dark with beard even when clean-shaven. He was no fool, and as John Hohner summed up the situation for him, all thought of whiskey and women left his mind.

Mentally, he began going over the herds he had passed on the way up from Texas, wondering which ones he dared visit on the way back. He had friends along the way, as did Mort Davis, but there were friends of both Steele and Lord among them, too. And

Davis was small potatoes when it came to the big out-fits.

He knew very well that one purpose of the oncoming range war was the avowed intention of the two big out-fits to possess themselves of Davis's ranch.

Davis's range was the best piece of grass from the Rio Grande to the Red . . . at least, in the minds of local ranchers.

The cowhand finished his coffee, wiped his mouth with the back of his hand, and got to his feet.

"Be careful," Hohner warned.

CHAPTER II

For those who opposed the stringing of wire on the range of Texas, the hour was late. Already, in a vacant lot in Botalla . . . and there were many such lots, for the town was very new . . . lay great reels of wire—gleaming spools of it ready for the stringing.

Reports had it that there was soon to be a railroad in Texas, and fat beef, good beef, was soon to be in great demand. If this should prove to be the case, then the long drive to Kansas and the railroad there would no longer be necessary, for the shipments could be made right from Texas.

The cattle would fatten on local grass, and the pos-session of good, well-watered range would mean wealth —almost immediate wealth, with the demand what it was.

Suddenly every rancher in the area began looking at his range with thoughtful eyes. And looking at that of his neighbor as well . . .

In the saloon of the Trail House in Botalla, rancher Webb Steele smashed a ham-like fist on the bar. "We're puttin' it up!" he declared, and Webb spoke always as if addressing a public meeting. "Hoss-high, pig-tight and bull-strong! If there's some as don't like it, and want war, it's war they want and it's war they'll get!"

"Who fences Lost Creek Valley?" Only a hardened soul could dare ask such a question. "You or Chet Lord?"

"I'm fencin' it!" Steele glared at once around the room as if he had expected a challenge. "If necessary, my riders will ride the fence with Winchesters!"

There was a murmur of subdued talk in the room, for such a statement was tantamount to a declaration of war, and everybody from the Neuces to the Rio Grande knew that when Webb Steele said he would fight, he meant it. They also knew that Chet Lord had never surrendered anything to anybody.

Nobody in his right mind made war talk in the Neuces Strip country unless he meant it. Those who ranched there were hard, tough men, accustomed to fierce fights with over-the-border bandits—many of them Anglos who took refuge in Mexico to avoid the law. Nobody wore a gun for show. There had once been a few of those but they had been buried long since, and those naive souls who might have ventured into the Strip were usually warned in time and rode away to more tolerant climes.

The rangy yellow horse with the black mane and tail—as well as three black ankles—sloped down the street toward the trail house, unaware and unconcerned. At the Trail House, the rider pulled up and swung down. He glanced at the lights from the windows, then tied his horse and loosened the cinch.

He stood for a moment, looking along the street. Then he hitched up his gunbelts and slipped the thongs from both guns.

He was a quiet man of rangy build, broad in the shoulders, slim in waist and flank, with a lean, brown face and green eyes. Leaving his dusty coat tied behind the saddle, he stepped up on the boardwalk and stood one moment longer. He wore a worn buckskin vest, black shirt and trousers, and a black, flat-brimmed hat. He was dusty and tired and, for just a moment before he stepped inside, he closed his eyes to clear away some of the tiredness in order to leave his vision clear.

He knew that the men along the walk—most of them seated at benches against the wall—had seen him. They knew him for a stranger. Their eyes had lingered a little longer than customary on the two tied-down guns. Two guns were only occasional, and tied-down guns were rare, for it was a method not much used and only of limited value.

He pushed through the doors into the saloon and paused just briefly to let his eyes adjust to the change of light. Webb Steele, brawny and huge, strode past him with the air of one who commanded the earth and all that was on it.

The stranger swept the room with a brief, comprehensive glance. It told him he knew no one there, and it was unlikely anyone knew him.

He walked to the end of the bar, away from the others. "I'll have a whiskey," he said.

Several men lounged against the bar, the nearest a young man who had moved into the place left by Webb Steele, a slim, wiry man better dressed than most cowhands, with black polished boots and large-roweled Mexican spurs.

The young man's cool gray eyes swept the stranger with a sharp glance. "Don't I know you?" he demanded.

The green eyes were expressionless. The stranger shrugged. "You might."

"Ridin' through?"

"Maybe."

"Want a job?"

"Maybe."

"Aren't you a cowhand?"

"Sometimes."

"We'll pay well . . . very well."

"What outfit are you with?"

"I am not *with* any outfit," the young man's tone was sharp. "I *am* the Tumbling R."

"Bully for you."

The young man's mouth tightened, and a queer kind of excitement came into his eyes.

"I don't like the way you said that!" His tone was aggressive, eager.

The man with green eyes looked at him, then looked away. He offered no comment, but the look was enough.

"In fact, I don't like *you!*" The young man insisted.

"Does it matter?" drawled the stranger.

There was an instant when the young rancher stared as if he could not quite believe what he had heard. Then he felt rather than saw the men hurriedly backing away from him, getting out of the line of any gunfire.

Something turned over inside the young man, and he realized with a sudden, sickening awareness that he was facing trouble, possibly a gun battle, out in the open and all alone.

With a shock he realized that he was frightened, that he had pushed himself into this situation of his own will. He felt an icy chill go down his spine. Always before, when he had talked loud and free or swaggered a bit too much, men had backed off because they knew he was Chet Lord's son. Men knew his hardbitten old father all too well.

The case of Bonner and Swindell had helped, too. They had affronted young Lord and both had been found dead on the trail, their guns in their hands.

Yet nothing his father might do later could help him now. He must fight. He stiffened, trying to seem unafraid, his mind scrambling like a frightened rat seeking a hole. Somebody would stop it, surely. Somebody *must*.

"Yeah, it matters, and I'll make it matter!" His voice shrilled a little, but his hand hovered over his gun.

The onlookers stared, tense, holding their breaths as one man. The tall stranger looked easily into Steve Lord's eyes, and then suddenly he smiled. There was humor in his eyes, not taunting or something worse, just plain good humor.

"Well." He spoke slowly, gently, "Don't kill me now. I'd hate to get shot on an empty stomach."

Deliberately, he turned his back and spoke to the bartender. "One more, and then I'm getting something to eat. Seems to me I ate half the dust in Texas for breakfast."

Everyone began talking suddenly, and Steve Lord, astonished at his good luck, turned to the bar himself. Something had happened, and he was not altogether sure what it was, but he suddenly knew he had narrowly escaped a shoot-out and with a man to whom such things were not new.

He faced the bar, thankful that the men on either side were strangers. He was trembling, if not outwardly. He was definitely trembling inside and could not trust his voice. He was going to have to watch himself. Since he was a child he had tried to adopt his father's hard, thrusting ways—but without what it took to back them up. He had always believed himself to be a tough, dangerous man and then, suddenly, in the first real showdown he had ever had with a stranger, all the sand had gone out of him.

Yet . . . why had the stranger turned away? He had heard his father speak of such men—men so sure of themselves that they could step casually aside. Yet a moment before, there had been death in the man's eyes, cold, ugly death.

Preoccupied with his own feelings and the shock that remained with him, he did not see what was happening. Only the stranger saw it, lifting his eyes from the just-poured drink to see a lean-bodied, thin-faced man slide quickly from his chair and go out a side door.

No one seemed to see him go but the stranger, who was the kind of a man who had learned to notice such things, to live with awareness, to recognize an enemy where others would see nothing but another human being. Too long he had walked the ragged edges of death, going quietly in where others shrank back. Only he had noted the hostility in the man's gaze, and the furtiveness he had been unable to disguise.

The stranger swallowed his drink, then turned quietly and went outside, unnoticed. For such minor altercations were not unusual, and there had been no shooting. Some would say that the stranger had backed down, others would realize that he had merely sidestepped a killing. But in any event it was over and nothing amiss had happened.

In the street, he paused. The thin-faced man was talking to three men who stood across the street in front of the Spur Saloon. He caught their eyes as they looked and sized him up, but he knew none of them. The trouble was, he was sure the thin-faced man had known him . . . or suspected him of being someone he *should* know.

He ought to leave town, and leave now, yet there were things he needed to know, and this was the best place to discover them. The stranger would wait a little longer.

Although he had not known the three men across the street, he had recognized their type. All three were cowhands, but the kind who relied more on what they could do with guns than what they could do with ropes or branding irons.

Idling in front of the stage station a few minutes later, he saw Steve Lord coming toward him. He knew him, as he had known Webb Steele from descriptions given him before he arrived in Texas. He was lighting a cigarette when Steve Lord stopped before him.

"You're a gunfighter," Lord said. "You could have killed me."

"Yeah."

"Why didn't you? I made a fool of myself. I was talking when I should have been listening."

The stranger smiled. "Why? Any man can make a mistake. You may be Chet Lord's son, but I think you can make your own tracks."

"Thanks. That's the first time anybody said that to me."

"Maybe they should have. Knowing you can act the man makes it easier to do it. And knowing it is expected of you helps. Many a man is brave just because people expect it of him."

"Who are you?" Steve Lord asked.

"Sometimes they call me Lance. Is that enough for you?"

"It's enough. And about that job. If you want it, we'd like to have you. I may not be so good with a gun but I know when another man is. And we want you on our side."

"I wasn't planning on going to work right now," Lance said. "I've got a few dollars and I'm figuring on taking it easy for awhile."

"Look, we'll pay well, and I'd rather have you on our side than the other."

"Maybe I won't ride for either side. This sounds like a shooting war you're talking about, and I've had enough of that for a long, long time."

"You've got to go one way or the other . . . or leave the country. I'm giving it to you straight. If you don't sign on with either side, one or the other will shoot you on sight, just suspecting you're riding for the others."

Lance shrugged. "Well . . . I don't know. What kind of a fight is this, anyway?"

"It's a three-cornered fight, not just two. Webb Steele has about forty riders . . . that's twice what he needs for the stock he runs. We've about the same number, and we don't need them all either, except as warriors.

"Between us, we split the Live Oak country. That's kind of a loose name for a big spread of country that runs from the Rio Grande to way north of the Neuces. Some folks name another section of country the Live Oak, but for us, this is it.

"It's always been a rough country, what with the border bandits on both sides stirring trouble, and Indians raiding into the area. Once this fight warmed up, a bunch of the boys began to choose sides, and some of them don't care who wins as long as they draw fighting wages."

"You said it was a three-cornered war? Where's the other corner?"

"He doesn't matter so much, no matter how you look at it. He's a squatter named Mort Davis. He came in here about three or four years ago and settled on a water hole near what they call Lost Creek. We cut his wire and he cut ours . . . Or somebody did.

"He doesn't stand a chance, caught between two big outfits like he is. He'll be wiped out."

"You squatted on your land, he squatted on his. What's the difference?"

Steve Lord stared at him. "You don't seem to understand Steele and Lord *own* this country. They came in here first, and they settled on it."

"And he came along later and settled on another piece. Strikes me that he's got as much right as you people have."

"Look, if we let every squatter who comes along settle on our land we soon wouldn't have enough left to graze a steer."

"But you didn't claim that land?"

"We did an' we didn't. That is, we claimed it but so did Webb Steele. Neither side had moved in there, both hoping to avoid a shooting war. Then Davis moved in. And then he brought in cattle from Mexico. That's a tough country to deal with down there, and he's a tough man."

"Heard something about that," Lance suggested mildly. "I heard Mort Davis bought the land from the Mexican who inherited it, that he paid cash for both the land *and* the cattle. It seems to me that if you attack a man under those circumstances, you're breaking the law."

Steve Lord shrugged. "What law?"

"Suppose he moved against you? I doubt if either you or Steele have filed on any land or have any legal claim whatsoever except squatter's rights."

"He only bought his from a Mexican!"

Lance smiled. "There are Mexicans who live in Texas, too, who have been citizens of the state from the beginning. There were Mexicans defending the Alamo as well as attacking it."

"I don't believe it!"

"Check on it and you'll see I'm right. Steve, if I were you I'd leave Mort Davis alone. You boys don't have a leg to stand on."

As he talked he was watching the street. Something was happening down there, something that smelled like trouble. The three men who had been watching him had been moving. One had remained about where he was, but the others had come closer, each taking a different side of the street.

"Steve," he spoke quietly, "you'd better get on down the street. I have a feeling I'm in trouble."

Steve turned quickly, puzzled, and glanced along the street.

"I'm not afraid." Surprisingly, he discovered that what he said was true. "I'll stay."

"Get out, Steve. Get out now. Thanks, but I don't want you here. Those men mean to kill me, and they might even be your father's men."

Startled, Steve Lord stared down the street, trying to make them out. Then suddenly he turned and ducked past an empty building.

The stranger who called himself Lance stood alone, waiting.

But then, had it not always been this way?

CHAPTER III

He started across the street toward the Spur. His only intention was to put them out of position, since they had obviously evolved some strategy. It was his way: never allow an enemy to fight in a situation of his own choosing: use whatever tactics necessary to throw them off balance.

He was halfway across the street when there was a sudden rattle of wheels and the pounding of racing hoofs behind him. He leaped aside just in time to escape being run down by a madly careening buckboard.

The driver—a girl—stood up, sawed the plunging broncos to a halt, then wheeled the buckboard in the middle of the road only to come racing back up the street. She jerked them to a halt alongside of Lance, and her eyes were blazing with anger.

"What do you think you're doing? Just standing in the middle of the street?"

She had come between him and at least two of the gunmen, and for a moment she had brought to a halt whatever plans they had.

Her red-gold hair blew in the wind, and her eyes were an amazing deep blue. She was beautiful, not merely pretty, but there was in her eyes the haughty disdain of a queen reprimanding a clumsy subject.

"Pretty," he spoke in a slow drawl, "but spoiled. Could be quite a lady, too." There was a tone of regret in his voice.

Then he smiled and removed his hat in an obsequious manner. "Sorry, ma'am. If you'll just let folks know when you plan to use the street for a racetrack I'll do my best to keep all the peasants out of your way."

Then he bowed again and turned to go.

"Wait!"

She took a couple of quick turns with the lines around the whip-stock, jumped to the street, and marched up to him. Her eyes were arrogant, her nostrils tight with anger.

"Did you mean to insinuate that I wasn't a lady?"

As she had leaped down from the seat, she had picked up a quirt, the type used when riding on horseback. It had by some odd chance been lying on the seat beside her.

He smiled again, but his eyes were serious. "I did,"

he replied quietly. "You see, ma'am, it takes more than beauty and a little money to make a lady. A lady is considerate of other people. A lady doesn't go racing around in a buckboard on a busy street. And when she almost runs somebody down, she apologizes."

As he talked, her eyes grew dark with anger, and the heat of her anger changed to the coldness of fury.

"You!" she said contemptuously. "A common cowpuncher trying to tell *me* how to be a lady!"

"Somebody should," he said gently.

She drew back the quirt suddenly and struck viciously at his face, but Lance was expecting it and he lifted his forearm, almost negligently, and blocked the blow. Then he dropped his hand over and jerked the whip from her hand.

The movement threw her off-balance and she fell forward into his arms. He caught her, looking down into her astonished eyes, blazing with frustrated anger, and at her parted lips. He smiled again.

"I'd kiss you," he said, "because it looks most inviting, and likely it would be fun, but I won't. Your kind kisses much better if you have to come and beg for it."

She tore herself free. "Beg?" Her eyes were blazing. "I wouldn't kiss you if you were the last man alive!"

"No, ma'am, I reckon you wouldn't get to. You'd be standin' in the line waiting, standin' away back toward the end."

A hard voice behind Lance cut the conversation short.

"Seems like you're takin' in quite a lot of territory around here, stranger. I'd like to ask you a few questions."

It was the thin-faced man, his thumbs hooked in his belt. Two of the other men had spread out, one right and one left. Another man was out of sight, behind him, no doubt. Or across the buckboard from him.

"Why, of course!" Lance said calmly. "Let's have your questions, and then I'll ask a few myself."

"I want to know where you was the day before yesterday."

Lance was puzzled. "The day before yesterday? I was riding, a good many miles from here."

"Have you got witnesses? You're going to need them."

"What's on your mind?" Lance felt the gathering of people about them, all listening.

"I suppose you'll claim you never heard of Joe Wilkins?"

At the mention of the name, there was a muttering from the crowd.

"You're right, of course," Lance agreed. "I've never heard of him."

"He was killed on Lost Creek Trail the day before yesterday. You were on that trail then, and there's some of us think you done him in. Do you deny it?"

"Deny it? I'm afraid I never heard of Joe Wilkins. I had no reason to kill him, and certainly do deny it."

"They found Wilkins," the thin man's eyes were on Lance, confident he had him where he wanted him, "drilled between the eyes. Shot with a six-shooter. You was on that road, an' he was carryin' money! You robbed him!"

Lance was thinking calmly. There was more behind the man's accusation than appeared on the surface. Either an effort was being made to force him to attempt a getaway—so they could kill him—or they were making an effort to discredit him. If he made a flat denial, it could be considered that he was calling the man a liar. This might trap him into a shoot-out. Yet what worried him most of all was the gathering crowd, none of whom knew him, and many of whom might have known Wilkins.

Lance chuckled. "How'd you know I was on Lost Creek Trail?"

"Because I seen you!"

"Then," Lance said gently, "you must have been on the trail, too. Or perhaps, since I didn't see you there, you might have been hiding off the trail. And if you were hidden in the brush, *why* were you hidden? Did you kill Wilkins?"

The man's eyes widened a little and there was a shadow of panic in them.

The crowd had expected Lance to say something that would provoke a fight. He was sure of that now—something that would make it possible for a legitimate killing. Instead, Lance had turned the accusation around on his accuser.

"No! I didn't kill him! He was my friend!"

"I never noticed you being so friendly, Polti," a big farmer interrupted. "If you were his friend, I figure you kept it a secret!"

Somebody laughed and Polti turned sharply. "You keep your mouth shut! I'll do the talkin' here!"

"You've talked enough," Lance said, "to make a man mighty suspicious. Why are you so anxious to pin this shooting on a complete stranger? Why were you hiding off the trail? No honest man needs to hide!"

"You killed Wilkins!" Polti insisted, and there was the look of sudden triumph in his eyes. "Everyone knows Wilkins had some gold dust he used to carry around. Here, I'll search those saddlebags you're carryin'! I'll show you!"

"You seem almighty sure." Lance kept his voice low and composed. "Did you put it in my bags while I was in the trail house?"

"Tryin' to weasel out of it?" Polti sneered. "Well, you won't! I'm goin' to search those bags here an' now!"

Lance held himself very still, but his eyes were cold. "No! If anybody searches those saddlebags it won't be you. But it will be done here, now, in the presence of these witnesses."

"I'll search 'em myself!" Polti declared. "Now!"

He turned, but before he could take a step, Lance moved. He grabbed Polti and spun him around. With a whining cry of fury, Polti went for his gun, but his hand never reached the holster. Lance's left fist clipped Polti's chin with a crack like that of a blacksnake whip, and Polti went to the dust.

"This don't look good for you, stranger," the big

farmer said fearlessly. "Let's just have a look at those bags!"

"Of course," Lance spoke quietly. "Although it wouldn't surprise me to find the dust there."

He led the way to his horse. Then, suddenly, he stopped. "No," he said, "a man might palm the dust if the sack is small."

He turned to the girl who had driven the buckboard. "Ma'am, my apologies for our earlier difficulty, and will you go through the bags for me?"

Her eyes snapped. "With pleasure! And I hope I find the evidence to hang you!"

She removed, one by one, the articles from the saddlebags. They were few and simple. A sack of .45-calibre ammunition, some cleaning materials, and a small coil of rawhide. Then a packet of pictures. And as she drew them out, one slipped from the pack and fell to the ground. She stooped quickly and retrieved it. She looked at the photograph. It was the face of an elderly woman, obviously a lady, and obviously, also, a person of dignity and poise. The girl glanced curiously at Lance, and then looked away.

"There is no gold here," she said quietly. "None at all."

"Well," Lance turned, "I guess—"

Polti was gone!

"Leaves you in the clear, stranger," the farmer said. "I wonder where it leaves Polti?"

"Probably planned to slip it into the saddlebags when he searched 'em," somebody said. "I wouldn't put it past him."

Lance glanced at the speaker. "That implies he has the gold dust. If so, he probably killed Wilkins himself."

Nobody said anything, but the crowd began to dwindle away. The big farmer shrugged. "Nobody can say that Jack Pickett lacks nerve," he said, "but I'm not going to tackle Polti and that crowd he runs with. They're gunmen and cow thieves, but it's not an easy thing to prove."

"You better watch your tongue, Jack," somebody said. "You've got a wife and family to think of."

Then they were all gone and only the red-haired girl remained.

"I'm still not convinced," she said. "You could easily have buried the gold dust."

"That's right, ma'am, I could have done that."

He turned his back on her then, untied the buckskin and walked away toward the livery stable. He walked because he wanted to think, and he thought pretty well on his feet.

He was beginning to have a rough outline of what was happening here. But where did Polti belong? On whose side was he? And why try to trap a stranger with no known ties?

Did somebody know for sure?

First, there had been a deliberate attempt to frame him—and then, no doubt, to kill him. Perhaps their first plan had actually been to stampede him into a gun battle. They had been boxing him in very neatly, to catch him in a crossfire.

He did not know Polti. Lance had neither seen nor heard of him before. Why was Polti out to get *him?*

Who could know why he had come to the Live Oak country and why he was in Botalla?

He had ridden in, had talked to no one, had scouted around a little to familiarize himself with the country, but had deliberately avoided human contacts and the possibilities of trouble.

The trouble seemed to have begun with his meeting with Steve Lord. It was then, so far as he knew, that the thin man had seen him for the first time, and yet the man had gone into action at once.

In the livery stable, a long and lofty building lined outside with stalls and corrals, he led the buckskin to a dark stall, then climbed the ladder to the loft and forked down hay.

There must have been thirty stalls to a side, and the stable smelled of hay and harness leather. Taking a handful of the hay, Lance proceeded to give the buckskin a good rubdown.

Suddenly a voice spoke from the darkness of a stall. "Busy little feller, ain't you?"

The speaker stepped from the shadows of the stall— a man with a battered hat, patched jeans and a hickory shirt. Powerfully built, he had brick-red hair, and a glint of humor in his eyes. His face was square-jawed and strong. He wore a six-shooter and carried a Winchester.

"I go by the name of Gates," he said. "They call me Rusty."

"I'm Lance."

Lance took Rusty Gates in with a quick glance. He knew the type instantly. Gates was obviously a cowpuncher, and the kind of man who was hard-working, honest and relatively fearless. Rusty was the sort of man to whom you could assign a job and then forget it, for the job would be done; perhaps even better than you had hoped. There were many such in the west, of all shapes and sizes, but all were men to ride the river with.

"So I've heard." Rusty squatted on his heels and began to build a smoke. "Like I say, you're pretty busy. You almost had a shootin' party with Steve Lord. Then you sidestep and let him off the hook. Some folks think you did that because you've decided to throw in with Chet Lord."

Rusty lit up. "Then you tangle with that wildcat of a Tana Steele—"

"Webb Steele's daughter? I might have known it. They're cut from the same mold."

"She'll never forgive you, friend. You took her too lightly. And nobody does that with Tana Steele. She's the queen of the Live Oak country and you'd better believe it. She'll get even somehow . . . She always does."

"What about Polti?"

"Bert Polti? He's a sidewinder. Kill you quicker'n scat. Always has money, never seems to do anything. He's mean, dangerous, and smart. He acted the fool with you, but then he didn't know *you'd* be smart. But don't underrate him. He's good with that gun."

"He hangs out at the Spur?"

"Mostly. Him an' that crooked outfit he trails with. Joe Daniels, Skimp Ellis and Henry Bates. They're a bad lot. And that bartender at the Spur is tough as a boot *and* a friend of theirs. Polti has connections on both sides of the border, and when the Rangers came in for a clean-up, he pulled his freight and wasn't seen around for months."

"I think I'll go talk to him," Lance said. "Straighten him out a little."

"Like I said, he's good with a gun."

"A lot of men are, I think."

Slow to anger, irritation had been mounting within Lance. Why should Polti choose him? Lance resented being pushed around. He always resented a bully, and Polti had made a deliberate move at him. And having failed once, it was unlikely he would stop. To avoid an issue had never been Lance's way, and he would not begin now. Move . . . Never let the other fellow choose the ground.

He left the livery stable and crossed the street to the Spur. Pushing open the doors, he walked in.

Rusty Gates was close behind him. "I just want to see this," Gates called out.

Lance had come to Botalla with a debt to pay, and had found the situation even worse than he expected— and even more serious for his friend.

With two big, aggressive outfits against him, he had small chance of surviving. And neither side seemed to have any thoughts on the real rights and wrongs of the situation. As Napoleon had said, and as the two sides believed, God was on the side of those with the most artillery.

Both Lord and Steele had big artillery . . . and so did Polti, And where did Polti stand?

A half-dozen men loitered at the bar and a couple were seated at tables when Lance walked in.

They may not have expected him, but they were ready . . .

CHAPTER IV

They turned and looked at him, their faces expressionless.

"Where's Polti?" Lance demanded.

One of the men who had been in the street with Polti was at the bar, another sat at a table, his legs stretched out, an expression of contempt on his face. Neither moved, and there was no reply.

"I asked, 'Where's Polti?' " Lance said, more sharply.

"You won't get any answers here, mister," the seated man said, his voice taunting. "When Polti wants you, he'll come to get you."

Lance took a quick step toward him, then glimpsed the flicker of triumph in the man's eyes and half turned his head to catch a glimpse of an upraised bottle, poised for throwing.

The man threw the bottle. Lance's pistol leaped from his scabbard to his hand and the gun roared. The bottle and fragments scattered.

Holstering his gun, Lance stepped in quickly before the shock of the sudden drawing and firing had reached the men. He caught the man by the shirt front. Jerking him into the punch, he threw his right fist into the man's belly. The unexpected blow knocked the wind from his body, and Lance shoved him away. Then he uppercut hard to his face, straightening the man up to take a fast left and then a high, hard one. The bottle-thrower hit the floor and rolled over. He did not get up.

The action had come so swiftly that not a single onlooker had moved. Spinning quickly, Lance kicked the outstretched legs of the man seated at the table, swinging his legs over and high. The man came off the chair and hit the floor on his rump with a thud that shook the building.

With no further hesitation, Lance stepped in. As the man gathered himself to rise, Lance kicked him in the face.

"I came in here," he said gently, "for a little polite conversation. But if you like it this way, you can have it."

Nobody moved. The first man down was beginning to groan. He tried to push himself up, then slid back to the floor. The man Lance had kicked was on his hands and knees, blood dripping from his nose in big, slow drops.

"You know," Lance continued, "the word is that you boys like to play rough. Now let me tell you something. You don't even know the name of the game. This is for babies. But if I have to, *I* can be rough."

He turned his head to look at the bartender, a thick-shouldered man who leaned with both big hands on the bar as if he planned to leap over.

"If you want to come over, Bottles," Lance said, "come on. They can always carry you back, if there's enough left to carry."

The bartender hesitated—and didn't jump. He was not afraid, but if he jumped there would be a moment when he was in the air, and he had seen how fast that pistol broke the bottle. Whether this man would use the pistol or his hands was a question, but the bartender decided he did not want to find out the answer. He stayed where he was.

"Now, once more. Where's Polti?"

"Apple Canyon," the bartender replied viciously, "and I hope you find him!"

Lance backed off. Then, seeing Rusty Gates at the door, his hand on his gun, Lance turned and went out, Gates following.

"For a stranger," Gates said, "you pick up country customs mighty fast."

"Where's Apple Canyon?" asked Lance.

"Apple Canyon is a draw that opens into Espada

Creek, right close to the border. That's where Nita Riordan hangs out her sign."

"Who's she?"

"Queen of the Border, they call her. Half-Irish, half-Mexican, and all wildcat. She's the best-looking woman in the southwest and a tiger when she gets started, but she's only a part of it. The other part is Jaime Brigo. He's a big Yaqui half-breed who can sling a gun as fast as the Brockmans. He can track like a bloodhound, and he's as loyal as a St. Bernard. Also, he weighs about two pounds less than a ton of coal."

"What is Apple Canyon? A town?"

"That it ain't. Apple Canyon is a saloon, dance hall, and a bunkhouse that'll sleep forty men. It is also a big barn, some corrals, and half a dozen houses. It is a place where the law never goes, where anybody passing across the border can rest up. And it's also where Bert Polti hides out when he wants to be alone —or when he's got some deal on both sides of the border."

"What's between here and there?"

Gates shrugged. "A few buzzards, a lot of rattlesnakes, more thick brush than you ever saw, and a scattering of centipedes, tarantulas, and scorpions. Everything that moves will bite or gore you, and everything that grows in the ground has thorns.

"There are trails through the brush, if you know where they are. And if you don't get lost and die there, you might, and I say *might,* find Apple Canyon.

"If you find Apple Canyon, you'll get yourself killed. Everybody down there is a friend to Polti except maybe Jaime Brigo, and nobody is a friend to outsiders, including Jaime Brigo."

"Tell me about Nita Riordan."

"First thing, she's straight . . . You try to lay a hand on her and you'll lose the hand—before they kill you. She runs a few thousand head on both sides of the border and nobody . . . but nobody . . . steals a cow with her brand.

"She owns and operates Apple Canyon. In her dance hall, she always has three or four girls—for dancing or conversational purposes only—and she operates the bunkhouse as a sort of hotel. And you pay and pay well.

"She can charge what she wants because it's either that or sleep in the brush. And you drink at her bar or you drink river water.

"Jaime Brigo works for her, and that's all. If she says 'Kill him,' he would. Anybody. He moves like a cat, and nobody wants any part of him.

"She has connections in Mexico City, in Saltillo and Monterey, as well as in Austin. Just what they are, nobody knows—*or* when she uses them, if ever."

"What's she doing in a godforsaken place like that?"

"That, amigo, is anybody's guess. I have no idea, and I don't think anybody else does. She's not a woman you put the question to."

"What's her connection with Polti?"

"None, I'd say, except that its a convenient station for him. I've been there a time or two, and far as I could see, she never even recognized the fact that he was there."

It was daylight when Lance started south, leaving Rusty Gates at the stable staring thoughtfully after him. He rode a trail that roughly followed the Neuces, then swung away toward the west, keeping to thick brush and working his way through it.

From trail to trail he switched, keeping his direction generally south by west, judging by the sun. In the thick brush he saw no one, then came out on the bunch grass levels beyond and rode at a somewhat more rapid gait.

The buckskin was eager to go, and by sundown they had covered more than half the distance to Apple Valley. Lance slowed his pace then, and at every chance checked his back trail. There was no sign that he had been followed, yet he took no chances. And at a suddenly-offered dim trail north, he turned abruptly north, rode a short distance and waited, listening. For some time he listened, but heard no hoofbeats nor other sounds of travel. If anyone was following, it would be

dark before they could reach this place, so he walked
his horse north, watching for a break in the brush. He
found it, rode into open, grass-covered country scattered with prickly peas—some of it towering as high
as a man—and rode on, quartering off to the west
again and just a bit south.

When the moon came up he found a small creek,
rode to a spot under some low-growing trees of a va-
riety strange to him, and there he watered the buckskin, let him have a roll, and then picketed him on the
grass. He bedded down there, and slept.

Twice he saw rattlers, but swung wide around them,
and once he startled a coyote drinking at a small pool.
He saw no man or woman anywhere. Then the brush
dwindled away and he rode through more or less open
country, riding with watchful eyes over some rough,
broken land with the Rio Grande off to the south—far
out of sight—but ever present.

In this country it was an omnipresent reality, for it
offered escape from the law for both Anglo and Mexican bandits—men who were prepared to commit almost any crime with such a refuge only a fast ride away
to the south.

Lance's thoughts returned to Bert Polti, in an effort
to seek some answer to the man's actions, yet he could
find nothing in his memory that might supply a reason. That the man was dangerous, Lance knew. That
he was prepared to kill and would kill, Lance also
knew. Yet why Polti's sudden decision to attack *him?*

Did he somehow represent a danger to Polti? Or to
some of the Polti interests? Did Polti know who and
what he was? Or surmise something of the kind *without*
knowing? Had Lance somehow been connected to Mort
Davis?

The impending sense of danger would not leave him,
and he found himself riding more and more slowly
despite the impatience of the buckskin, who loved a
trail and wanted to go, to get on with the journey.

There were many arroyos now, low cliffs and dry
streambeds. There were occasional thickets, open
prairies, and patches of prickly pear or mesquite.

The place worried him, as did the events since his arrival at Botalla. There was more here than the smile on Steve Lord's face, and the sullen anger of the lovely but pampered Tana. There was death here, and the smell of gunpowder. Not the death of bold men facing each other over drawn guns, but the death of the dry-gulchers, the men who lay in wait to ambush and kill.

Was this merely another range war, or was there something else?

Well Lance knew what the threat of barbed wire on the range could do. Cattle ran free now. They were separated and divided at roundups. But there were men here who had no cattle, yet did a bit of branding quietly and, hopefully, without being seen. With fencing, that would end. With fencing, the big cattlemen who could afford to buy wire would fence vast acreages, squeezing out all others. And their fences would be patrolled, as Steele had promised, with men carrying rifles.

It was public land, but who was prepared to enforce it against the big cattlemen?

The small outfits, starved for range, saw their livelihoods threatened, for few small ranches were paying propositions. These outfits were angry, and many would fight back. Yet what might happen was apparent in what had already happened to Joe Wilkins.

The small men had no money to hire gunmen. Many of them had no money for wire. Squeezed off the big range, they would have to graze their cattle on less and less land. And, what was worse, most of them would be closed off from water, and without water, land was of no value.

Fences had been cut. Men rode the range armed and ready, and many a small rancher, although alone and unaided, was still a man to be feared. His gun spoke as loud as that of the big rancher, and often he was a former soldier, Indian fighter, or buffalo hunter—a man to whom battle was no stranger.

It was a time when men shot first and asked questions later. It was a time when Sam Bass and his outlaw gang rode the trails, John Wesley Hardin was running up his list of killings, and when King Fisher, in this very area, had a gang said to number more than five hundred men on both sides of the border. King Fisher, it was said, had chaps made of tiger skin and a sombrero loaded with a silver band, with silver-plated, pearl-handled six-shooters.

There were several hundred known outlaws operating in Texas, and another five hundred known outlaws in New Mexico, not too far to the west. All these men rode with guns. It was the accepted way of settling disputes, recognized as such in the eastern states and in Europe as well.

From the crest of a ridge, Lance looked over what was called Lost Creek Valley and saw the silvery strands of barbed wire stretching away as far as the eye could reach. Yet the Lost Creek country needed less wire than most, for the sheer cliffs along the canyons protected much of it, and there was water. From his vantage point above the valley, Lance could see why they all wanted Lost Creek. The water supply was more than sufficient, and the grass was good. It was prime grazing in any man's country, a piece of land to be desired and defended.

"I don't know, Buck," he said to his horse. "I don't know about this wire business. It does give the nester a chance to raise a crop, and it gives the rancher a chance to improve the breed. And anybody can see that the longhorn is on the way out.

"You an' me, Buck, I think we're on the way out, too. We're free, and we can go where we want, but we don't like fences very much. Maybe we'd better ride north for Dakota. Wyoming. Or even Canada or the Argentine."

It was late evening when the sure-footed mustang turned down a narrow trail among the brush and boulders. This was no honest man's trail, but Lance knew the nature of the man he rode to see—a man who would never be less than honest, but who would fight to the last for what was rightfully his.

The trail dipped into a hollow several hundred yards across, and when he was halfway across the hollow,

Lance saw what he wanted. Dismounting, he led his
horse to shelter behind a boulder. Sitting against a rock,
he watched the declining sun fall slowly westward,
watched the shadows creep up the walls and the sunset
splash the cliffs with crimson . . .

He must have fallen asleep, for when he awakened
the stars were out and Lance judged several hours
to have passed.

It was very still, and for a moment he did not move,
sitting quietly, listening to the night. It was then that he
saw the gleam of starlight on a pistol barrel. It was
aimed at him from across a rock. But even as he
moved, the pistol's muzzle flowered with sudden flame.
He heard the thunder of the shot; he heard the bullet
strike. And in almost the same instant, he was struck a
vicious blow from behind and fell forward on his face
in the grass. As consciousness faded he seemed to feel
something long and sticky on his cheek. . . .

A long time later he felt a throbbing pain in his
skull, as if a thousand tiny men were pounding with
red-hot hammers at its shell, pounding and pounding
and pounding without cease.

He opened his eyes to a star shining through a crevice
in the rock across the hollow, and then he saw something long and dark lying on the ground. Something
. . . like the body of a man.

Painfully, Lance rolled over and got his hands under him. Yet it was several minutes before he mus-
tered the strength to rise, to push himself up from
the ground. He found that he had difficulty in bringing
his eyes into focus, and he sat with his head leaning
on his arms, crossed upon his knees, for what seemed
a long, long time.

At last he lowered a hand to the rock at his side.
Then another. With difficulty, his head swimming,
Lance pulled himself to his feet. Once on his feet, with
the flat face of the rock for support, he dropped his
hands to feel for his guns. They were still there.

Apparently the body had then been left for dead.
Gingerly, Lance's fingers went to the man's skull. His
hair was matted with blood.

Feeling around on the ground, Lance found the man's hat and let it hang from his neck by the rawhide chin strap, for his head was too sore and too swollen to permit his wearing it. Feeling his way around the boulder, Lance found Buck waiting patiently. The yellow horse pricked his ears and whinnied softly.

"Sorry, boy," Lance whispered, "you should've been in a stable by now, with plenty of oats."

When he led the horse from behind the boulder, Lance again saw the dark shape on the ground. He saw more than that, for just beyond was a standing horse.

Gun in hand, for he knew not what awaited him, Lance went over to the body.

By the feeble light of the stars he could yet see the man's features, and it was the face of no one he knew. Then he saw the white of a bit of paper clutched in the dead man's hand. He freed it . . . An envelope.

Squatting, his head pounding with slow, heavy throbs, Lance struck a match. It was a worn envelope. It must have been carried in a man's pocket. On it was scratched in a painful scrawl:

> *I was dry-gulched.*
> *Mort needs help bad.*
> *He koodn't kum.*

It was written on the back of a letter addressed to SAM CARTER, LOST CREEK RANCH.

Thrusting the letter into his pocket, Lance mounted and rode down the trail toward the ranch. He was close now, judging by the description he had, yet obviously Mort's enemies had staked out along the trails to get anyone who might try to come in or out.

He turned from the trail when he saw an opportunity, and let the buckskin scramble up a steep bank to the top. This was open country, but away from the trail. He had been sent a map to indicate his direction and the ranch location. A few added comments from Rusty Gates had helped immeasurably.

Lance was still several miles away when he saw

the glow of fire on the horizon, the blaze of burning ranch buildings.

He was too late. A house was burning, and perhaps Mort Davis was already dead.

Suddenly a man ran from the shadows. "Is that you, Joe?" he called.

Lance drew up sharply, waiting. The man came closer. "Joe? What's the matter?"

The voice was that of one of the men with whom he had fought in the Spur. They recognized each other in the same instant that something fell in the burning house, and the flames leaped up.

With a startled gasp the man lifted his gun, but Lance held his Winchester on him. And without shifting the rifle, Lance squeezed off his shot.

The gun bellowed in the night, and the man pitched forward, clutching his stomach.

"That's one less, Mort. One less."

He touched a spur to the buckskin, and rode on, toward the dying fire.

CHAPTER V

Lance walked his horse toward the dying fire, his rifle in his hand. Had they killed Mort? Had his ride of more than a thousand miles been for nothing?

In that time, so much could have happened. Lance had so little real understanding of the problem. The wire, he felt, had only been the match that had lighted the fuse, for the trouble must have been long in developing. Neither Lord nor Steele were men to settle for second best, and to the cattleman in Texas his way of life was the only way.

Years before the Texas ranchers had settled here,

gathering vast acres when the value of land was nothing
—or existed only in the minds of visionaries. They
were empire builders, sure of their own rightness, their
own place in the march of progress. And their em-
pires were of grass and beef—but the possession of
these was nothing without water.

Nesters were men who came in and plowed up the
grass they needed, who settled on water holes or springs
they had come to regard as their own. And a small
rancher was to them a species of thief, a man who,
having no cattle or very few, increased their small
herds with a vagabond branding iron. At the same
time, the big ranchers were rarely scrupulous about
what cattle they branded.

Often the small rancher did not even own a bull.
He let his cows roam the free range, profiting from the
bulls owned by the big ranchers . . . So there was at
least a basis for much of the big ranchers' argument.

Wire was to change all that. It was to fence in range,
to deny water holes to those who did not possess them,
and deny free access to range bulls. The cattlemen who
could afford to would now buy better bulls and improve the breed.

Lance knew something of the story of Lost Canyon.
The canyon had been avoided by most of the big
ranchers because of its proximity to Mexico, and because it had been for some years a hideout for cattle
and horse thieves. The year-round springs were a lure,
but the few times cattle had been left there they had
disappeared. Yet both Lord and Steele considered that
the canyon belonged to them . . . They had just not
taken final possession. And when one of them tried,
they would settle it between them.

Mort Davis had moved in, settled on the land, and
brought in his cattle from Mexico. He was a tough
man who would stand for no nonsense. Both Lord and
Steele were irritated. Each had tried in his own way to
push Davis off, but Mort Davis had been pushed before and stood his ground. Only when Steele and Lord
began to fence across his opening—and to import gunmen—had Davis sent for help. And only, Lance knew,

when Mort's own hands had been driven off . . . or killed, like Joe Wilkins, who occasionally worked for Davis.

Lance rode slowly toward the fire, keeping to the deepest shadows along the edge of the brush. Suddenly, from near the flames, he heard the bark of Mort's old Sharps .50, and the several shots fired in reply.

Lance glimpsed movement near a tumbled adobe wall. Quickly touching the buckskin with his spurs, Lance charged and leaped the wall, firing into the group as he went over, racing on a dead run for the flaming house.

A man loomed up before him, pistol cocked to fire. It never did. Reins in his left hand, Lance fired the Winchester like a pistol at almost point-blank range.

The man's eyes widened in the horror of death, and he toppled back as Lance's horse went by, bullets whistling about.

Mort was crouching in the shadows near a bulky corral post, and Lance leaped from his horse, sending the animal dashing into the doubtful shelter of a small barn.

Turning as he lit, Lance began firing as fast as he could work the lever on his rifle. He saw men break and run for their horses, and he nailed one of them. He saw another stagger. Dropping the Winchester, he came up with both guns, firing them alternately.

Then the firing ceased, and sudden quiet descended. Lance began to thumb cartridges into his guns, one at a time. Holstering them, he picked up his Winchester and reloaded.

Mort Davis got up slowly, stiffly. "You sure take your time, Lance," he said, grinning. "Why couldn't you have been here when the fight started?"

"What? And deprive you of all the fun? You old wolf, you don't need help. You just want somebody to talk to. That's what comes of living alone, Mort Davis."

The dark-bearded man clapped Lance on the shoulder. "Lance, I'd nobody else to turn to. When I heard the Brockmans were comin' in, well . . . I'm all right with a Sharps, Lance, but I'm no match for their kind."

"They're good . . . very good," Lance agreed seriously. "Are you sure they're here?"

"No . . . just heard it."

"Who were those fellows?"

"You got me. Could have been some of Steele's men, or Lord's." He scratched the stubble on his jaw. "Let's have a look."

A gangling sixteen-year-old strolled down from the rocks. He carried a duplicate of his father's Sharps.

Three men had been left behind, and with the man Lance had killed further out, it came to a total of four. It had been a costly attack, but they should have known better than to tackle Mort Davis.

"Don't look like anybody I know," Mort commented. "Course, they been hiring new hands."

"Pa," the boy said, "I seen this one in Botalla, trailin' with Bert Polti."

Lance studied the man's face. It was not one of the men he had previously seen.

"Mort," Lance said slowly, "if the Brockmans are in it, who are they riding with?"

The older man shrugged. "I don't know. Abel used to work for Steele, one time, but he took to hangin' around Tana, and the old man let him go. Abel Brockman didn't like it much, either."

"It doesn't look right," Lance said. "Everybody is talking about Steele and Lord, and even they are talking fight talk, but so far the only fighting I've seen seems to come from Polti's men. They jumped me in town, and without any reason that I know of."

"You watch them Brockmans," Mort warned. "They work as a team and they've got it worked out to a science. I mean, they always corner you so's you can only get one at a time under your gun.

"They're tough and they're mean, and they hunt trouble. At one time or another they've been into ever' fuss there's been that I know about. They like the extry pay, but it ain't that so much as that they just like trouble."

Lance glanced around. "They didn't leave much, did they? Is there any place you can hole up for awhile?"

"Well, we got us a little cave back yonder. We lived there for a spell before we built the house, and we're used to makin' do. I mean, we never had much, so we're used to doin' without. If we can keep this land we can be well fixed in a year or two, with me and the boy workin' it ourselves."

"You'll keep it," Lance said quietly, "or else I made a long ride for nothing."

Mort Davis had done much to make the west a fit place in which to live, and he was getting old now and deserved the rewards of his years. Neither the big outfits nor any gang of outlaws were going to drive him out if Lance could prevent it.

"Who knew that Sam Carter was to meet me?" Lance asked.

"Nobody I know of. He's a puncher who started a little herd over west of here. He was just settin' down to supper with us when the shootin' started and I asked him to find you."

Lance described the nature of his trouble in Botalla, and added an account of his run-in with Tana Steele.

"I'd given a purty to've seen that," Mort said, chuckling. "She's had her head for a long time. Drives that buckboard like a crazy woman! But she's quite a girl. She can ride anything that wears hair, and she will! Best lookin' woman around here, unless its Nita Riordan."

"She's the woman who runs Apple Canyon?"

"She is. She runs that shebang all by herself. Well, almost. She has that big Yaqui around, and nobody wants any part of him."

They talked a little longer while Lance helped Mort and his son carry what was left of their goods to the cave. It was a good position, hard to approach and easily defended.

"You hole up and stay out of trouble, Mort. I've got some riding to do."

It was very late and Lance was dead tired, but he had managed to catch a little sleep before the trouble started, and he needed more information before he could begin to understand what was happening here. He must talk to Lord and Steele, and try to stop trouble before they could begin a shooting war.

Four men had died, but not one of them was in any sense a key character in the drama. They were simply men who carried guns and used them for hire. And dozens more could be found to take their places.

Yet Sam Carter was now dead, and no country could afford to lose such men: A cowpuncher who had gumption enough to set up for himself and to fight for what he believed in. No man such as Mort Davis would turn aside from an honest way.

On the inspiration of the moment, Lance turned the buckskin and headed for Webb Steele's outfit. He could lose nothing by talking to Steele, although the role of peacemaker was not one to which he was accustomed. Yet if peace were not made, the two cattlemen were going to blunder into a war from which neither could gain.

That idea turned him thoughtful. If not them, then who? The two old fire-eaters were ready for war, and yet neither seemed to have actually done much but blow fire and brimstone. What had been done was done by other parties. Who was paying them, and who stood to gain if the two big outfits slaughtered each other?

Mort?

Lance hesitated over that . . . How well did he know Mort, after all? The man had saved his life. He seemed to be an honest rancher. But suppose he was not? Or suppose he had been, and had recently taken a dishonest step to grow rich quick? Or quicker?

Lance was well into the Steele ranch yard before a man with a Winchester stepped from the shadows.

"All right, stranger! Keep your hands steady. Now step down easy-like and walk over here."

Lance obeyed without hesitation, carefully keeping his hands in sight in the light from the ranch house window. As he approached, the other man stepped farther from the shadows—a slender, wiry man whom

Lance instinctively liked. Obviously a cattleman, he had the mark of the range upon him, a face seamed and brown, yet kindly beneath the sternness.

"Who are you?" the man demanded.

"Name of Lance. Riding by and figured 1 should drop in and talk to Steele."

"Lance?" Something sparkled in the man's eyes. "You the gent had the run-in with Miss Tana?"

"I'm afraid I am that man. Is she still sore?"

"Lance," the older man chuckled, "as sure as I'm Jim Weston, you've let yourself in for a packet of trouble. When that gal rode in here, she was fit to be tied! You got a nerve to come here after that! I'll be surprised if she doesn't shoot you on sight." Then his manner changed. "What do you want to see Steele about?"

"Stopping this war. It doesn't make much sense."

"What's your dicker in this? A man doesn't do nothin' lest he's got a stake in it somewhere."

"What's your job here, Weston?"

"Foreman. Why?"

"What's the ranch figure to make out of this war? And what will you make from it?"

"Grief, an' trouble an' headaches, an' not a cussed thing else. We got all our punchers guardin' fence when they should be handlin' cows. We're losin' cattle, losin' time, and losin' wire. I never knew anybody to gain anything from a range war, anyhow, but the old man's not about to be backed down by anything or anybody."

"My feeling exactly. I don't like it either. My own angle is Mort Davis. Mort's a friend of mine. And, Weston, I mean to see that Mort keeps his place on Lost Creek. He'll keep it if we have to plant a few bodies around every tree on the place."

"Think you're pretty salty, do you?" Weston suggested, but there was a glint of understanding in his eyes. After all, he and Mort Davis might have been cut from the same mold. "Well, maybe you are."

"I've been around, Weston, but that cuts no ice. You and me can talk. You're an old trail hand and you're a cattleman, and you're too smart to let pride blow this country wide open. Just what have you got against Mort Davis?"

"Nothin'. He's a sight better hand and a whole lot better man than lots of them ridin' for this here ranch right now. I know what you mean, but I don't make the rules for this ranch right now. Webb does . . . or Tana."

"There's been killing enough," Lance replied, "I don't want any more."

"You mean Joe Wilkins?"

"I mean Wilkins and Sam Carter—"

"Carter's dead?"

"Killed on the trail tonight . . . dry-gulched. Four others died, too. There was a fight at Lost Creek."

Weston had been walking toward the house with him, now he stopped. "Whose hands? Not ours?"

Lance shook his head. "It's a puzzle, Weston. There's more going on here than either Steele or Lord knows. Those men belonged to neither ranch, but young Davis said he'd seen one of them with Bert Polti."

"Polti? I don't figure that."

They had entered the ranch house and stopped at an inner door. Weston rapped. At a summons, he opened it.

Big Webb Steele was sitting tipped back in his chair on the other side of a big table. His shirt was open two top buttons, showing a massive, hairy chest. And his hard, level eyes seemed to pierce Lance through and through. On his right, in a big easy chair, was Tana. As she saw Lance she came to her feet, her face taut with anger.

A tall, handsome man in a plain black suit was there also, a man with blue-gray eyes and a neatly trimmed blond mustache.

"*You!*" Tana burst out. "You have the nerve to come here?"

Lance smiled, and he had a pleasant, friendly smile. "I didn't reckon you carried your whip in the house, ma'am. Or do you carry it everywhere?"

"From what I hear, young man, you've taken a high hand with my daughter." Steele glanced from Tana to Lance and back. "What happened between you two?"

"She seemed to be trying to use the main street for a race track, and when I got in the way she was going to horsewhip me. I sort of explained to her it wasn't exactly lady-like."

Steele chuckled. "Young man, you're in trouble. I will say you've got nerve. But I let Tana fight her own battles, so let heaven have mercy on your soul!"

Lance shook his head gravely. "You mentioned me taking a high hand with your daughter, but if my hand had been applied where it should have been, it might have done a lot more good."

Webb Steele's eyes twinkled. "Young man, I'd give a hundred head of cattle just to *look* at the man who could do that!"

"Father!" Tana protested. "This man insulted me!"

"If you don't mind, ma'am," Lance suggested, "we can continue this discussion another time. I've come to see your father on business."

Tana's face flushed and she started to speak but Lance had turned his shoulder to her. He took a seat.

"Mr. Steele," he said, "I've come in the role of peacemaker. You people here are edging yourselves into a three-cornered war that's going to cost plenty in cattle, time, and men, to say nothing of cut wire and gunpowder. I'd like to set up a meeting between you, Chet Lord and Mort Davis."

"*Davis?*" Steele let the legs of his chair down hard. "That no-account nester will make no talk with me! He'll get off that claim or we'll run him off! You tell that damn highbinder to take his stock an' get!"

"He's caused trouble here." The stranger with the blond mustache interposed. "Cutting fences and that sort of thing. He's a menace to the range." Then he added, "I'm Victor Bonham, from New York City."

Lance merely glanced at him, then turned his attention back to Steele. "You have the reputation of being a square shooter, Steele. You came west with some damn good men, and you've made a place for yourself. Well, so did Mort Davis, only he went further west than you. He went on to Santa Fe and Salt Lake City, and he helped open this country up. Now he finds a nice piece of land and settles on it . . . What's so wrong about that? And isn't that what you did?"

Lance shifted his chair a little, then went on. "He fought Comanches and Apaches. He built a place. He cleaned out the water holes and did things in Lost Creek you'd never have done. And there'd have been no trouble between you if this fencing hadn't started.

"It seems to me that Mort is just as entitled to stay on his land as you are on yours."

Lance leaned forward. "Steele, I haven't been in this neck of the woods but a few days, but it takes no longer than that to see there's a lot going on here that I doubt either you or Chet Lord knows anything about.

"Mort Davis was burned out tonight, and by orders from somebody. And I don't believe those orders came from either you or Lord.

"I want Mort Davis let alone, and if you and Lord are so damn hot for a fight, then have at it, but leave Mort out. Or," Lance's tone softened a little, "I will have to take a hand in the fight myself."

"You talk very loud for a loose-footed cowhand," Bonham put in. "We just might decide not to let you leave here at all!"

Lance saw Tana glance over at him, startled. Even Webb Steele seemed surprised.

Lance merely glanced at Bonham. "I don't know where you fit into the picture, Bonham, but when I get ready to leave a place I usually do."

"Better leave him alone," a new voice interrupted, "I think he means what he says."

It was Rusty Gates, standing in the doorway, rather pleased at the effect he had created, surprising them all.

"I was ridin' by, thought I'd stop in and rustle a cup of coffee. But just take a friendly tip."

Bonham started to speak, but Gates interrupted.

"Better shut up, New York man," Gates said. "There's been enough killing tonight. If you keep talking you're likely to say the wrong thing."

Rusty smiled suddenly, and threw an amused glance toward Lance. "You see," he was lighting a cigarette, "I've heard Lance Kilkenny could be might touchy about what folks said of him!"

CHAPTER VI

The name dropped like a bomb. Tana's hands went to her throat, and her eyes were wide and startled. Webb Steele's chair legs hit the floor again and his big hands slapped the table. Jim Weston backed up a little but, of them all, he seemed the least surprised.

Oddly, it was Victor Bonham, the man from New York, whom Lance Kilkenny happened to see at that moment. And he saw an expression of startled fury that vanished so suddenly as to make him believe that it might have been an hallucination.

"Did you say *Kilkenny?*" Webb Steele demanded. "The gunfighter?"

"My name is Kilkenny. I've never sought a reputation—with a gun or without one. Mort Davis happens to be a friend of mine, and I do not forget my friends when they are in trouble." Lance glanced over at Steele. "I didn't come in here hunting trouble, but Mort was attacked and his place was burned."

"What happened?" Bonham asked.

"Four men were killed. None of them were men anybody could recall working for either Lord or Steele. But Mort is still alive and in good shape, and I intend to see he stays that way."

"If so many people are involved," Bonham commented, "it doesn't seem likely that one man can make much difference."

"Sometimes, Bonham," Kilkenny commented, "one man can make all the difference."

"Mort Davis burned out?" Steele shrugged. "Well, he'd no business there in the first place. I'd not have done it, but he got what he asked for."

"The question you might ask yourself, Steele," Kilkenny said, "is who burned him out, and why? You and Lord are pulling and pushing at each other to see who's the biggest man, but while you're doing it I'd suggest you think about who else has a finger in the pie.

"You and Lord think you're ruling the roost. I think somebody is setting you up as a scapegoat. You and Lord will bluster around and make a fine show of things, and if you aren't very careful you'll find yourselves out in the cold, wondering what hit you."

"Is that a threat?"

"No, it is not. I never make threats, nor have I any place in this fight except to help my friend."

"Wasn't there a story about Davis nursing you when you were sick? Or helping you through some kind of a bad time?" Bonham asked.

"There was."

Kilkenny turned back to Steele. "You and Lord should get together with Davis, as I suggested. If you do, you'll have peace around here."

"You handle your affairs, Kilkenny, I'll handle mine. When I need advice from you, I'll go to you for it."

Lance Kilkenny shrugged. "Your problem, Steele. I have nothing to lose. You have everything to lose and nothing to gain. Good night."

Lance rose, went out the door and down the steps. Tana Steele was standing beside his horse. He had seen her when she left the room, but had not expected to see her here . . . or ever again.

"So?" Her voice was scornful. "I might have known it! A common gunman! A man who shoots down others less capable than he!"

"At least," he smiled at her, "I give them a chance. I don't run over them in the street."

He paused. "You know, ma'am, you're right pretty in the moonlight, where nobody can see the meanness in you. You've either got a streak of real devil in you to come out here just to say something unpleasant, or else you're falling in love with me, and I don't know which worries me the most!"

She stepped back angrily. "In love with *you?* Why, you conceited, contemptible—"

Lance had stepped into the saddle and turned the horse as she spoke. He bent quickly and scooped Tana up with one arm and kissed her soundly on the lips. Her lips responded almost in spite of themselves. But then he dropped her and rode off, singing:

> *Old Joe Clark has got a cow*
> *She was muley born*
> *It takes a jay-bird forty-eight hours*
> *To fly from horn to horn.*

It was an old song, a good song, and he felt like singing.

Tana Steele, quivering with anger or some emotion less easily understood, stood staring after him. She was still staring as his voice died away in the distance.

In less than forty-eight hours she had had a whip taken from her, had been threatened with a spanking, had been ignored, treated carelessly, told she had a streak of meanness in her, and that she looked pretty in the moonlight. She had also been swept off her feet and kissed soundly, kissed more thoroughly than at any time she could remember . . . and for such things her memory was very good.

She told herself she hated him, but her reasons were vague and unsound, and even in her own mind the statement had a hollow ring.

He was a gunfighter, a killer. A man known wherever western men gathered. How many stories had she heard of this man? The mysterious man who came from nowhere, and whom no man really knew—and who, after his killings, disappeared into the limbo from which he came.

Disappeared? Would he do that again? Where had he come from? Who was he? What was he? Where was he going?

She remembered the picture she had picked up of the elderly woman. Certainly, no average woman, no common woman. There had been both beauty and distinction in that face, the face of a cultured woman of the world, a woman of breeding.

Why would Lance Kilkenny carry such a picture? His mother? His aunt?

She remembered the dress, too. It was a dress from an earlier period, but fashionable for its time.

Who *was* Lance Kilkenny?

There was a movement behind her and she saw Rusty Gates swing into his saddle to follow Kilkenny.

"Rusty?"

He drew up. "Ma'am?"

"Who is he?"

"Kilkenny, ma'am? Everybody knows who Kilkenny is, even those who've never seen him. He's a gunfighter, ma'am, perhaps the fastest, deadliest man alive when it comes to a good gun battle."

"I don't mean that. I mean where does he come from? What *was* he?"

Rusty considered for a moment. He was restless and eager to be off. But the question was one he had often wondered about himself. "I don't know, Tana," he said frankly, "and I don't believe anybody else does either."

He lifted a hand and rode out of the yard, turning down the trail Kilkenny had taken.

Tana Steele stood alone then, looking into the night. She was puzzled and angry. It irritated her that there had been no immediate final answers. She was also disturbed by her own feelings, telling herself the man was a nobody. Probably an outlaw; no doubt vicious and dishonest. She told herself this, but she didn't for one moment believe it. There was a certain quiet distinction about Kilkenny that spoke of breeding . . . The man had come from somewhere; he had been somebody.

Jim Weston came up to her. "Anything wrong, ma'am?"

"No, Jim, nothing." Then she added, "That man worries me."

"Kilkenny? Well, if Webb goes after Mort Davis, you've got cause for worry. If Webb leaves him alone, you haven't. It's that simple. I never heard of Kilkenny killin' anybody that wasn't askin' for it. Usually, nobody even knows who Kilkenny is until the moment before he dies. Often enough he'll just ride into a place under some other name, and he'll punch cows or something of the kind and bother nobody. He's a top hand . . . rides like a man born true to the saddle, and he's an expert with a rope. Plus he's not quarrelsome . . . never stirred up any trouble I know of."

"Well! I'm surprised, Jim. You talk as if you were on his side."

"Didn't know there *was* any sides yet, ma'am. You asked and I answered. And I gave you an house opinion."

"I'm sorry, Jim. I know you did. I'm just not myself tonight."

He turned and looked at her. "No? Somehow I thought you were."

He walked away, and she stared after him, half-angry. Now what had he meant by that? She wondered.

It was several minutes before Rusty Gates caught up with Kilkenny. He found him waiting in the shadows, a Winchester in his hands.

"What do you want, Gates?"

Rusty leaned forward and patted his horse on the neck.

"Why, I reckon I want to ride along with you, Kilkenny. I've heard you were a straight-shooter, and I guess you're the only one I know who can get into more trouble than me without tryin'."

"If you can use a good man by your side, I'd admire

to ride along. I've a feeling that in the days to come you could use some help."

"All right, Rusty. Let's ride."

When Lance Kilkenny rolled out of his blankets in the earliest dawn, he glanced over at Gates. The redhead was still snoring. Kilkenny took up his boots and shook them thoroughly to be free of any scorpions and tarantulas which might have taken refuge there during the night. Grimly, he contemplated a hole in his sock.

No time for that now. He pulled on his boots and stood up.

Carefully, he checked his guns.

Then he moved out from camp, keeping under cover, and for fifteen minutes he made a painstaking search of the area. Not until he was sure nobody was within the immediate vicinity did he lead his buckskin into camp and saddle up.

Lance and Rusty were encamped on a cedar-covered hillside with a wide view of Lost Creek Valley. Lance mounted the buckskin and rode quietly away, but he was back and had bacon frying before Rusty Gates awakened.

Coffee was bubbling in the pot when Rusty came over.

"Hey!" Rusty exclaimed. "You've got bacon!"

"Picked it up last night from the Mexican who gave us the frijoles. He's got half a dozen hogs."

"Hell, man, if he can get a half dozen more he's got the key to the mint. Bacon is scarcer than minted gold in this country!"

Rusty rustled some wood for the fire, then saddled his horse. When he returned to the fire he squatted on his haunches, feeding sticks into the flames.

"How about this Bonham?" he asked suddenly. "Have you ever seen him before?"

"No." Kilkenny paused a moment, then said, "How about you?"

"No. He ain't from around here."

"I wonder."

"You wonder? Why? They said he was from New York City and he surely dresses like a pilgrim."

"I agree to that, but you were curious yourself, Rusty. And he knew about Mort caring for me when I'd been shot."

"Hell, that story's been told time and again. Everybody knows about that. Just like they do about that supposed meeting between John Wesley Hardin and Bill Hickok. Stories like that are told around every camp fire. And every time you hear them, they're different. You're just too suspicious."

"I'm still alive," Kilkenny commented, dryly.

"You've got something there." Gates walked to the edge of the nearest cedar and picked some dead stuff off the ground to bring back to the fire. "Who do you think he is?"

Lance shrugged. "No idea." He turned the bacon over. "Except that my name got a rise from him. I thought I caught a look in his eyes . . . Well, no matter. Maybe I was seeing things."

They were silent for awhile, listening to the bacon frying and enjoying the tantalizing fragrance as well as the smell of the burning cedar.

There were a few clouds in the sky that looked like rain, and occasionally the wind stirred the fire, blowing the flame.

"You came up with something last night when you implied this fight wasn't simply Lord and Steele."

"Do you think it is?"

Rusty shrugged. "Well, you started me thinking. We had all sorta taken it for granted that it was Lord and Steele, with one or both of them planning to rub out Mort Davis in the process. But if it isn't just them, who is it? Who else is there?"

"You've been in this country longer than I have, Rusty. Who stands to gain, aside from them? Suppose they both get killed or their outfits get so crippled they can't stay on top. Who wins then?"

"Nobody. Those two have got it all sewed up.

There's nobody close around who stands to gain anything . . . except maybe Mort Davis. If they got out of
his hair, he might spread out himself."

"Ever look at a map of this country, Rusty?"

"Map? Hell no. I didn't know there was one. Who
wants a map?"

"Maps are handy things, my friend. Sometimes you
never know what a country looks like until you've seen
it on a map. A bird's-eye view can change a lot of
things for you. A big country like this has a way of
looking different on a map, and you can't get a good
idea of the relationship of one place to another without
one. Look here."

Squatting on his heels, Lance Kilkenny drew with
his finger in the sand.

"That V," he suggested, "represents the combined
holdings of Lord and Steele." Off to one side he drew
in Lost Creek Valley. He indicated the valley with his
finger. "Right where Lord and Steele's holdings come
together is Lost Creek Valley.

"That's what the fuss is about," said Rusty. "They
both want the valley and they both want the water."

"I know. But look here . . . All this country that
Lord and Steele control runs from the point of the V
right into the widest cattle ranges in Texas.

"Up there are other cow outfits, many of them with
far greater holdings than Lord and Steele combined. I
rode through that country on the way down here, and
saw some of the finest stock I've seen, with a lot of
white-face bulls that have been brought in to improve
the grade of beef.

"In a few years this is going to be some of the finest
stock-raising country in the world. The fences won't
make much difference, except to limit the size of the
roundups. The stock will be better, more beef to the
hoof than before, and there'll be a bigger demand for
the better beef.

"The small ranchers won't be able to afford better
bulls, and here and there they'll cut fences as much to
let the bulls get at their own stock as anything. But
that's only one small part of it."

Rusty was paying close attention.

"Look at those vast miles of good range that lay north of Lord and Steele. That range will be covered with fat stock, thousands of head that will feed the range off little by little. They won't be allowed to over-graze if the cattlemen are smart, and can be shifted from one area to another as the grass is eaten down to give the rest of the grass a chance to grow.

"Now most cowhands have rustled a few head—or at least been a little careless how they use a running-iron. A man works for the outfit, and if he finds stock on his boss's land he brands it . . . It's not supposed to be that way, but many a small outfit grew big just like that.

"Look here." Kilkenny drew a line with his finger in the sand, a line that went from those vast ranges to the north down through the Lord and Steele range and into the country below.

"See?" he asked.

Rusty swore softly. "Sure enough, I do."

Rusty put a finger on the crude map. "You mean whoever wound up holding Lord and Steele range could rustle cattle and take them right through to Mexico? What you're tellin' me is that whoever held Lord and Steele range could do as he damn well pleased, could appear to be honest ranchers with never a head of rustled stock on their range, yet profit from all the rustled stock?"

"It's a possibility," said Lance. "And right now it's the only answer I can see to what's happening."

"And Bert Polti's involved?"

"Seems so."

They ate the bacon from the frying pan, strip by strip. For several minutes both were busy with their thoughts, but Lance Kilkenny got up then and walked away from the fire to listen.

It looked like rain, and they had some distance to go, yet he was in no hurry. He would be expected to be early on the trail, and if there were any hidden marks-men along the route they would begin to sense that he had taken another route.

He and Rusty had a long ride before them, but one they could manage well enough. He had learned long since that it was better to vary his time and pattern of travel as well as his route. Vigilance was the price of life, and not only of liberty.

He walked back to the fire. "There's a lot of border down there on the Rio Grande, but look what's at the point of the V that I drew?"

"Apple Canyon?"

"Right . . . And it's a hangout for outlaws. It's one of Bert Polti's favorite places. The Lord and Steele ranches, with Apple Canyon, would provide a safe route for rustlers over the last forty or fifty miles of their drive. That route could be a huge funnel pouring stolen cattle into Mexico."

"What do we do now?" Gates asked, as he began cleaning the frying pan.

Kilkenny spread the remains of their fire and kicked dirt over it, then threw the last of the water and the coffee over the coals that remained.

"Why, we mount up and ride down to Apple Canyon. We just go down and have a talk with this woman . . . What did you say her name was?"

"Nita Riordan," Rusty said. "And wait until you see *her!*"

CHAPTER VII

Their route lay south and west, along trails rarely ridden except by outlaws or smugglers. It was a country covered with clusters of oaks surrounded by grassy plains, the brush and trees like islands in a sea of coarse grass, prickly pear and other low-growing stuff.

It was a dangerous country through which to ride,

with the clumps of oaks, brush and occasional arroyos. For any one of these could be an ambush. There was a trickle of water here and there in some intermittent stream that emptied into the Rio Grande, but water was scarce and much of it brackish.

The buckskin took easily to such country, ambling along naturally, accustomed to having his head and going at his own pace when on a long trail.

Rusty Gates, his face burned almost as red as his hair, rode behind Kilkenny at times, and then in front. It was easy to admire a fighting man, and Kilkenny had a position in the hard land of their living that few men could equal. The army knew him as one of their best scouts. The Indians had fought against him or beside him, depending on the circumstances. Always one to admire a good fighting man, Rusty Gates had done his own share of it, fighting when necessary because it was natural to him. It came more easily to him than to most.

He had been about everywhere in four or five states and territories where a man could go on a horse. Like Kilkenny, he rode much alone, taking jobs where he found them, occasionally riding shotgun, driving stage, herding cattle or freighting, but he preferred the cattle business. Twice he had started small spreads himself, and once he had sold out and gambled away the money. Another time, he had been dry-gulched and then driven out, so he understood the plight of Mort Davis.

It was a hard land, but he wished for no other. Nothing in his years had been easy. Rusty Gates had grown up on a small farm, milking cows, making hay, cutting wood, caring for stock and trying to make a crop from land that was far from the best. He had worked with his father and then when his father had been killed in the Kansas troubles, he had gone on, supporting his mother and his four younger brothers and sisters.

His mother had died when he was sixteen, working to make ends meet. A year later, Rusty had lost a sister to the cholera, and one brother was killed by a bad horse. Another brother, at fourteen went to work on a riverboat, and his sister, at sixteen, married a doctor in Joplin. At nineteen, Rusty rode away west to find what fortune might offer. He wanted land of his own, a few head of horses and cattle. Along the way west, then up and down the cattle and stagecoach trails, he began hearing stories of Wild Bill Hickok and John Wesley Hardin, of Billy Brooks and Jack Bridges, of Mysterious Dave Mather, Bill Longley and Cullen Baker.

There were other stories, too, of Cochise and Crazy Horse, of Satanta and Mangas Colorado, of the death of Jedediah Smith and of Lieutenant Harrison, killed by Indians with whom he was trying to be friendly.

There were stories about Ben Thompson and King Fisher, who hailed from this country where he now rode. But there were few stories about Lance Kilkenny.

There might be trouble, a gun battle, a man—or men —dead . . . and Kilkenny gone. Some thugs tried to rob him in a gambling den in Abilene. Two of them died very quickly. The others had backed off, wanting no further trouble.

He had been cornered by Kiowas in a buffalo wallow —and left three dead, one wounded, and took the gun from the last man and set him afoot to tell the story to his people. Two weeks later he had stopped three tough white men from abusing a Kiowa boy, bought him a horse and sent him to his people carrying the rifle he had taken from the fight at the wallow.

But the true stories were few, the man himself elusive. Many talked of him, but descriptions varied. None seemed to be altogether accurate. Before the shooting started, he attracted little attention. And after it was over, when men would have been able to take a good look at him, he was gone.

Some said he had killed eighteen men. The cattle buyer in Dodge claimed the actual figure was twenty-nine. But all of it was talk and nobody knew for sure. Not being a tinhorn, Kilkenny filed no notches on his guns.

"You know," Rusty said suddenly, "the Brockmans hang out at Apple Canyon."

"I know," Kilkenny agreed. "And we may run into them."

Rusty Gates bit off a chew of tobacco. "There's better places to tangle with them than in Apple Canyon. There'll be fifty men there, maybe a hundred, and all of them friends of the Brockmans."

Kilkenny grinned at him, whimsically. "What are you worried about? You've got fifty rounds, haven't you?"

"Fifty rounds?" Rusty rolled the tobacco in his jaws and spat. "Shucks, man, I miss once in awhile." He threw a speculative glance at Kilkenny. "You seen the Brockmans? You're a big man . . . must weigh one-ninety or better, and either of the Brockmans will out-weigh you by forty pounds! And I seen Cain Brockman shoot a crow on the wing!"

"Did the crow have a gun?" Kilkenny asked, slyly.

That, Rusty decided, was a good question, a mighty good question. It was one thing to shoot at a flying target, another when the moving target was shooting back.

They circled a stand of brush and drew up in the shade. "Let's let him catch up," Kilkenny said.

"Catch up? Who?"

"Steve Lord. I picked him up a few miles back."

"You mean to say you can see that well?" Rusty stared back over the way they had come. "I can barely make out it's a man!"

"Look again. Lord has a hatband made of polished silver disks that catch the sun, and he rides straight up —like a military man . . ."

Rusty rolled his quid and spat again. Easy enough, he reflected, when you know how. Now that it was mentioned he remembered that hatband. He had seen it so many times it no longer left an impression.

"By the way," Kilkenny said, "I want the Brockmans myself."

"*Both* of them? Listen, I—"

"Both of them," Kilkenny replied. "You can keep the sidewinders off my back."

The distant horseman was closing the gap. Kilkenny took off his hat and ran his fingers through his damp hair. He glanced again at the clouds. Broken here and there, but a promise of rain.

"About that Mendoza deal. I was in Sonora right after you took him. They said he was the fastest man in the world with a gun, yet you beat him. Did you get the jump or were you just faster?"

"Didn't amount to much, but he did beat me to the draw."

"I didn't think anybody ever beat you," Rusty said.

"Several men have, and he did. It may be he saw me a split second sooner. Fact is, I think he did."

"How come he didn't kill you?"

"He made a mistake. He drew faster, but he missed his first shot. He didn't get another."

A faint breeze stirred among the oak leaves. Kilkenny looked again at the approaching rider. It was Steve Lord, all right, but why here? At this time?

They rode on, taking their time, watching the approaching rider as well as the trail ahead.

Steve Lord came up at a gallop, reining in when he recognized Lance. He glanced sharply from one to the other.

"I didn't know you had interests down this way," he said.

"We're takin' a look at Apple Canyon," Rusty said. "An' I want to introduce Kilkenny to Nita."

Steve glanced at the gunfighter. "I heard somebody say that you were Kilkenny, but I didn't believe it. You don't fit any of the descriptions."

"Just as well," Kilkenny commented. "I'm not anxious to be known."

"I should think you'd—" he paused. For the first time it dawned on him what Rusty had said. "What's your interest in Miss Riordan?"

"None at all," Kilkenny replied. "Rusty is showing me the sights, and from all I hear, she's one of them."

"She is beautiful," Steve agreed, "but I'm not sure she would appreciate being considered one of the 'sights.' "

"No offense meant," Rusty said cheerfully. "But any man who wouldn't ride a hundred miles just to be in the same room with her is no kind of man. She's a *woman!*"

Kilkenny glanced at Steve, who obviously agreed but was somewhat disturbed by this talk about her. Was he infatuated? Well, it would not be surprising. He was young, very good-looking, and obviously very concerned with himself.

"You know, Steve," he suggested, "I had a talk with Webb Steele last night. And if we're going to avoid a war that will do nobody any good, we've got to get your father and Mort Davis together with him."

"*Mort Davis?*" Steve exploded. "Why, Dad's threatened to shoot him on sight! They'd never dare get in the same room!"

"I'll be there," Kilkenny commented grimly. "And if there's any shooting done, I'll do it."

Steve was doubtful. "I'll talk to him, but it won't do any good. He's pretty hard-headed."

"So's Webb Steele," Rusty added, "but we'll bring him around."

"Did you ever see a cattle war, Steve?" Kilkenny asked.

"No, I never did," he admitted. "But we heard about the Sutton-Taylor fight and the trouble between the Regulators and the Moderators."

"Well, then you know how many men can die. Most younger men think they're going to live forever, but there's no guarantee of that. The young can die as quickly as the old, and if there's a shooting war started you'd be sitting up there as a first-rate target. And nobody's even going to hesitate about shooting."

"I'm not afraid," Steve protested.

"Not now . . . Nobody is shooting at you. Surprising how quick a man's feeling can change when lead starts flying. Because a bullet doesn't care who it hits. A man always has the idea that it's the others who will die, not him. But all the dead men thought that, too."

"You think that? *You . . . Kilkenny?*"

"Of course," Lance said simply. "Any man is vulnerable. And I think a man who knows he can die is a more dangerous antagonist than one who believes he cannot. Fearlessness is often the very thing that gets a man killed."

"Anyway," Rusty said, "why fight when it's in somebody else's interest?"

Steve turned sharply around to look at him. "What does that mean? Whose interest?"

Kilkenny let his horse walk on a few steps before he replied to the question. Rusty had made a sort of gesture implying, that he should explain.

He glanced over the country before him from a bit of a rise. He was riding into unknown country and he did not really like traveling with others. Any conversation was distracting, and to one who lived his kind of life, such distractions could be a matter of life and death.

Yet the years had tuned his ears for the slightest sound—and his eyes to any change in the terrain, or any flicker of light or dust.

"Because somebody else is involved," he said then. "Somebody who wants Lord and Steele out of the way, somebody who stands to win a good deal if they kill each other off or weaken themselves for him to move in.

"Your father and Steele think that they are the movers and shakers of things around here, but they aren't. They are being moved like a couple of pawns on a chessboard—and for the advantage of some player whom we do not know."

"I don't believe it! That's all poppycock!"

"The fact remains that the men who killed Sam Carter and Joe Wilkins, and the men who attacked Davis the other night, were not either your men or Steele's. Find out who is behind those shootings and you'll find out who is stirring up this fight."

"You won't find anybody at Apple Canyon who knows anything about it," Steve Lord said irritably. He looked from Lance Kilkenny to Rusty Gates. "And you'd better watch your step! The Brockmans are there!"

Steve Lord suddenly spurred his horse and rode rapidly off down the trail ahead of them.

"Now what's bitin' on him?" Gates asked.

Kilkenny shrugged, but he had an idea. Yet as he rode he was not thinking of that, but of himself—something he rarely permitted. Beyond seeing to the few essential details of living, he lived a Spartan existence, and he permitted himself few luxuries, few friendships. It was a hard and lonely life, one that had grown more so as he had grown older, for the life of a man known to be good with a gun is never a secure one, never an easy one.

There were always the few would-be tough kids who wanted to prove something, and Lance avoided them, for he had nothing to prove. He had never wanted to be known as a gunfighter. It had simply happened to him.

In a land and a time when all men carried weapons, and when they were essential to survival, some men were killed by those guns. It was, and had been for many years, the accepted manner of settling disputes, not only in the west but in the east as well.

Nor was it only in America that insults or disputes were settled with weapons, for it had been the practice over most of the world, recorded since time began. Senators and Congressmen, members of the cabinet and generals, captains and midshipmen or warships, all had settled their disputes with swords or pistols. In the west it was simply more casual, more offhand, less formal.

Yet in a land where all men carry weapons, some men are sure to be more skillful and adept than others. Some have that dexterity in handling a pistol, that coolness of nerve and steadiness of hand that allows them to win when gun shots are exchanged. And after a few of these battles, a man would become known. If he emerged a victor three or four times, he was certain to be considered a "gunman" or "gunfighter." It was as simple as that.

Kilkenny had known many, and among them were lawyers and gamblers, doctors and businessmen, cattlemen and farmers. Oddly enough, except for the few who had been outlawed for killing the wrong man or killing too many, few of the men who were on the dodge were actually gunfighters. Among cow thieves and bandits, really good men with guns were few.

His own case had been like the others. He had been hunting since childhood, had grown up with guns and respected them. He had no desire for reputation. Yet there had been certain difficulties, certain situations, and he had won. He could use guns as few men could—two guns at once, yet it was something he rarely did.

What was happening hereabouts he had seen happen elsewhere, and he knew it would happen over and over again in the years to come. Struggle was the law of growth, and the west was growing up the hard way.

The very nature of the men involved made such troubles inevitable. Each was strongly individualistic, each was proud, and each demanded respect. They were strong men living a rough life, taking on in the process much of the culture of the Indian through whose land they were passing or settling. The Indian warrior was also a proud man, with his own standards of behavior, and his status as a fighting man was all-important.

In the immediate fight that Lance Kilkenny saw as inevitable—unless something could be done immediately—good men would die. And the west needed its strong men. And here in this wild borderland, such men were even more essential.

As for himself, he was tired. Young in years, he had ridden the long trails for much of his life, and knew only too well what such a fight entailed.

He had wanted none of this, but Mort was a friend, a man who had risked his own life when Kilkenny was in trouble. And being the man he was, Kilkenny could do nothing else but come to the help of Mort Davis.

And then another long trail, and perhaps death at the end. That was always the way.

CHAPTER VIII

There was much that was familiar about this ride. He had taken many such rides into unknown country, with known trouble at the end.

He knew all about the Brockmans. They were huge, enormous men, muscular and strong. They were feared as fist-fighters as they were with guns, aggressive and quarrelsome rowdies in their own country and here. They picked fights, hunted trouble, and often hired themselves out as thugs or gunmen.

Huge as they were, and skillful with weapons, they went about where they liked and did as they pleased, approaching the inevitable time when they would cross the wrong man and die. Sooner or later, it always came.

It had been the way of Kilkenny to go right to the heart of any trouble, and Apple Canyon looked to be in the very center.

Lance did not underrate Bert Polti. The gunman was quick as a cat, as dangerous as a weasel. He would kill and kill until he finally went down. He would kill from ambush, but there wasn't a cowardly bone in him. He would simply kill in the most efficient way. He had faced many men with guns and no doubt he would again, if that was the only way.

Neither Webb Steele nor Chet Lord were killers. They were rough, tough men, a bit on the bullheaded side, no doubt, but probably kindly men on most occasions. Lance had known many of their kind, and in fact, Mort Davis was very much like them in every sense.

Bert Polti, however, could only be a tool. His was

not the mind to plan what seemed to be happening. He was a keen-edged tool, but a tool nonetheless. Whose tool he was, Kilkenny could not guess.

Whoever was behind this was a man or woman relentless and evil, someone with intelligence and skill, someone who knew the country, the situation, and the elements involved.

Someone also, who knew Lance Kilkenny. Or knew about him.

Above all, somebody who did not fear him.

If he came out of this alive there would once again be the long night rides, the scant food, brackish water, and the harsh living of the fugitive—or one who was almost that—and then a new attempt to find new peace in new surroundings. Sometime he might succeed, but sooner or later his past always seemed to catch up with him.

Several times he had considered leaving the west and going back east, but he was no longer fitted for that life. The skills needed for life in the east had left him; his knowledge of their ways had been blunted. Nor could he bear to leave the lands of immense distances, the purity of the air, the vast sweep of the mountains, plains and forests, the smell of his lonely campfires, the feeling of a good horse under him, and the song of the lonely winds. It was in his heart now, in his blood and bones, and in all the convolutions of his brain. Lance Kilkenny was a western man, and he would stay a western man until one day on some lonely mountainside, or on some lonely western street, he would die with a bullet in him.

Even now he was in danger. By now the person he opposed, a man or woman unknown to him, would be aware that he had taken cards in the game, and the greatest risk lay not in what Steele or Lord might do, but what he, Kilkenny, would almost certainly do.

He must force the play. He must keep moving. He must try to get his enemies off-balance. His approach to Steele had been the real beginning of this ride to Apple Canyon.

The direct attack. It was always best with the plotter, the conniver, the adroit man. Such a man wanted time in which to plot, to make his moves upon the board, and the best way was simply to keep pushing. To attack, always attack, until the unknown man was forced to reveal himself and come out into the open.

Kilkenny had foiled such plots before, but could he break this one?

Looking over the situation, he realized he was not entirely sure. His enemy was cool, deadly, and dangerous. Knowing Kilkenny, while he himself was not known, he could see or anticipate Kilkenny's moves. And, from the shelter of his ghost-like existence, could hunt him down . . . or have him hunted.

Kilkenny looked thoughtfully at the country before and around him. Without doubt this would be an easy route by which to take cattle into Mexico, and if one man controlled the way south, he could appear an innocent rancher, with no stolen stock ever appearing on his range.

With millions of cattle on the range in Texas, many could be stolen and taken out of the country before anyone realized what was going on, and then if due precaution was taken to cover the trail left by the moving cattle, it might be months, even years before it was realized.

It was midafternoon when the two riders rounded a rocky bend and looked down the street of the rickety settlement of Apple Canyon, so named because of an orchard once planted, and now almost gone.

There were four buildings on one side of the street, three on the other.

"The nearest one is where the doc lives. He's a mighty good sawbones, but a renegade from somewhere and some*thing*. Next is the livery stable and blacksmith shop, all in one. That long building next door is the bunkhouse, and Bert Polti's place is just beyond. He lives there with Joe Deagan and Tom Murrow."

"On the right side is Bill Sadler's. Bill is a gambler. He did a couple of stretches for forgery, and he'll cook up any kind of documents you want. Right alongside is the big joint of Apple Canyon . . . the Border Bar. That's Nita's place and she runs it herself.

"The last house, the one with the flowers, is Nita's. They say no man has ever entered the place." Rusty glanced at Kilkenny. "Nita's straight, though from time to time some have had their doubts. Nita soon sets 'em right on that."

"And the place on the hill beyond the town?"

"Huh? What do you mean?"

Kilkenny pointed. On a rocky hill beyond the town, in a place that seemed secure from all but circling eagles, he could dimly perceive some kind of a structure. Even with the sunlight falling on the cliff it was but a suggestion, yet as he looked he could see a flash of light reflected from something.

"Whoever lives there is mighty careful," Kilkenny commented. "He's looking us over with a field-glass."

"I'll be damned!" Rusty was disgusted. "I been here three or four times an' stayed five days once, and I never knew that place was there!"

Kilkenny nodded. "I'll bet a pretty penny it can't be seen from the town. I'm just wondering who it is that wants to be so careful? Who is it who watches all who come to Apple Canyon? Who can manage to live up there and remain unknown?"

"Do you think—?"

"I don't think anything yet. There's just somebody up there with a glass, far as I know. But I'm a kind of curious man, Gates, and I mean to find out."

He glanced right and left, and spotted a dim trail off to the right. "Let's just kind of circle around, Gates, and keep something between us and that man up there."

"Take a good rifleman to hit anything that far, and especially when we're so much lower down."

"But he might be a good rifleman, Gates, and he might have fired some test shots at one time or another. I think I'll suppose he could cover the entering of the town from up there."

"What are we going to do?"

"Ride right in . . . but not on the trail. We'll just

circle those rocks and hit the street from back of that barn."

They turned their horses and rode down through the rocks by a dim trail obviously made by cattle and into the arroyo, then across it into the mesquite that lay beyond. Kilkenny led the way, and he took his time.

Of course, they had seen him, and of course they'd be ready for him. But he didn't believe they'd try to dry-gulch him as he rode into town.

He walked the buckskin past some old corrals and the barn and then turned into the street.

They came in together but Kilkenny was a dozen paces in the lead as the two men rode slowly along the street. A man sitting in front of the Border Bar turned his head to say something through an open window, but aside from that there was no immediate movement.

A man loafing in front of the Border Bar had a rifle in his hand. And in the rocks at the end of the street there was another. "This ain't just for us," Rusty commented. "This here's the way it is. There's some folks hereabouts who don't wish to be caught with their chaps down."

At the hitching rail, Kilkenny swung his horse and stepped down quickly, rifle in hand. He looked across his saddle at the man loafing by the window. The fellow was a sandy-haired man with a rough look about him, but a half-humorous glint in his hard blue eyes. "Howdy," he said. "You boys passin' through?"

"Depends on the climate. Maybe we'll set a spell."

"Gets right chilly around here sometimes," the fellow said cheerfully. "Right chilly. I've heard some folks just can't stand it."

"Well, now. Do tell." Kilkenny grinned at him. "Lucky I brought my gun along to keep me warm, ain't it?"

"Lots of guns around here, amigo. Big ones and little ones. They don't count for much, most times."

"Here an' yonder I've found things warm up considerable," Kilkenny said, "given the chance. Seems a right nice little valley, and the folks here seem to be mighty friendly, country-like people. I figure I could probably get to like it."

"Your funeral," the puncher said, shrugging.

Kilkenny grinned at him again. "Most generally," he said, "it isn't." And he walked inside, letting the doors swing to behind him.

Rusty Gates paused on the walk. "Travelin's a dry business," he commented.

"Risky, too, when you're in the wrong comp'ny. You're askin' for trouble comin' here with him. The words out."

"They better take it in again," Rusty replied shortly. "As for me, I'm ridin' with him."

"On your own then. Can't help you none."

"Ain't asked. Now you just stay out of the way."

Rusty stepped inside to see Kilkenny standing at the bar. The bartender was idling down the bar, doing nothing, paying no attention.

In a deceptively mild voice, Kilkenny said, "I'd like a drink."

The bartender did not move, nor give any indication that he had heard.

"I'd like a drink," Kilkenny said, just a shade louder.

Three men seated in the room were covertly watching. Two of them sat against the south and west walls. The third man was across the room almost directly behind Kilkenny and against the east wall. The bar covered most of the north wall except for a door at each end that led into rooms back of the bar.

"Once more," Kilkenny suggested mildly. "I'd like a drink."

The burly bartender walked nonchalantly down the bar. He stared at Kilkenny with hard eyes. "I just don't hear you, stranger. And I don't know you."

What happened then was to make legend in the border country. Kilkenny's hand shot out and grasped the bartender's shirt collar in a tight grip and jerked ... hard enough to bring the bartender right over the bar and to the floor, where he sprawled in the sawdust.

"Let's get acquainted," Kilkenny said mildly, and as the bartender came off the floor he lanced his cheekbone with a straight left. A right to the chin made the man's knees sag.

Before he could recover his balance, Kilkenny grasped his shirt front and landed a stiff uppercut to the windpipe that made the man's mouth drop open, then pushed him away and hit him in the face with both fists. Kilkenny stepped back. The bartender slid toward the floor, caught at the bar, and tried to pull himself up.

Kilkenny watched him and said quietly, "Now we know each other, don't we? Get back of that bar and let's have a drink for myself and my partner. Or you can have the second barrel."

As the bartender started to weave toward the end of the bar, Kilkenny turned. Rusty was standing to one side of the door facing the man against the east wall.

Kilkenny glanced at the other two. "The name is Kilkenny." He paused a moment to let the name sink in. "If you want me, turn loose your dogs."

The name rang like a challenge in the room, but the three men made no move. The gunman against the west wall put a nervous tongue to dry lips. In his own mind he was sure of one thing, and one thing only. If they went through with their plan he himself was sure to die. No one had warned him the man they were to face was Kilkenny.

The name had caught all three of them flatfooted. They stood deathly still, their faces stiff with shock. Slowly, the man against the south wall began letting his hands ease away from his guns.

"Now that's over," said Lance (the bartender was spilling whiskey as he poured their drinks), "let's talk a little. It was mighty nice of you folks to welcome us like this, but how can I express my feelings about it unless you tell me who sent you?"

"We weren't going to kill you," one man said, "just make you a prisoner."

"Sorry, boys, I just don't take to becoming a pris-

oner. Now you know where Mexico is, so why don't
you just head on down that way before I get nervous
and go to shooting?"

The three men headed for the door and ran into the
street.

Kilkenny turned toward the bar. The bartender had
stepped back, the bottle in his hand, listening.

There was a shot, then two more. Kilkenny stepped
over to the window and looked out.

One man was halfway across the street, sprawled in
the dust. The other two had just stepped off the stoop
when they were hit.

"Who the hell did *that?*" Rusty asked.

"Seems their boss doesn't like failure," Kilkenny
said.

He walked back to the bar. The bartender was sitting down, holding his head in his hands. They were
shaking.

"If we want more drinks," Rusty commented, "I
guess we'll have to pour them ourselves."

"That won't be necessary." It was a smooth, lovely,
feminine voice.

CHAPTER IX

A girl stood at the end of the bar, facing them.
She stood erect, her chin lifted a little, one hand resting
on the bar. Her skin was the color of old ivory, her
hair jet-black and gathered in a loose knot at the
nape of her neck. But it was her eyes that were most
arresting, her eyes and her mouth.

Her eyes were hazel with tiny flecks of a darker
color, and they were very large, her lashes long. Her
lips were full, but not too full, and they were beautiful.

Yet despite her obvious beauty there was a certain wistfulness in her expression, a certain elusive charm that prevented the lips from being sensual.

Her figure was seductively curved, and she moved with a sinuous grace that had no trace of affectation.

She came up to them and held out her hand to Kilkenny. "I am Nita Riordan," she said simply. "May I pour you a drink?"

Kilkenny looked into the most beautiful eyes he had ever seen, eyes that looked strangely into his as if searching for something lost. "Nita Riordan," he said gently, "you could indeed."

Taking up the bottle she poured two drinks and handed one to each of them. She did not even glance at Big Ed, the bartender, who was beginning to move about.

"It seems there has been trouble," she said calmly.

"No more than any man would willingly encounter to meet a girl like you," Kilkenny replied.

"You are gallant, senor." She looked directly into his eyes. "Gallantry is always pleasant, and especially pleasant here, where one finds it so rarely."

"I'm only gallant when I am sincere," Kilkenny said. "And I say little for effect."

She glanced at him—a slow, level, curious glance as if anxious to find something in his face. Then she looked away.

"Sincerity is difficult to find in the Live Oak, senor. It has little value here."

"It has value to me anywhere." He glanced at Big Ed, who was now somewhat recovered. "I don't like to fight, but sometimes it becomes necessary."

"Now that," she said coolly, "is not sincere! No man who did not like to fight could have done *that!*" She gestured at Big Ed's face. "Perhaps you like to fight, but you do not like *having* to fight. There is a difference, you know."

"There is," Lance agreed, "and it is to avoid having to fight that I have come here. Nita Riordan, who is the man in the house on the bluff?"

She hesitated, then shrugged slightly. "If there is such a man, senor, why do you not ask him?"

"I'm afraid he has no intention of giving me the opportunity, senorita," Lance said. "But he seems very interested in all who come to Apple Canyon."

He paused. "Why is it called that?"

"I am told there was once an apple tree planted here . . . or several of them. There are other stories, too, but that is the accepted one.

"It was, for some time, a very lonely place. For nobody came this way, and the route to the border was untraveled except by occasional Comanches or Apaches. To most travelers it is out of the way, off the beaten track, and they have no reason for coming. Yet it is, after all, only one of many routes across the border."

"But an almost hidden route," Lance added. "One could come to Apple Valley if one wished, by devious routes, and remain unseen. One might even drive stolen cattle or horses this way without it being known."

"Perhaps you are right, senor. I only live here, and what others do does not concern me."

"The law does not concern you?"

"What law? This is a border settlement. Is it Texas law? The law of Mexico? Or the law of survival? I believe the law of survival is the oldest of them all, senor, and I wish to survive . . . at least, up to this point."

She gestured toward the street, where the bodies of the three men had been removed. "Survival is not always easy, senor, and you saw what happened to the three who failed in their mission.

"I do not wish to die. There is much joy in living —even here, where there are only outlaws and thieves. Yet even here the world can be bright, even here one can find a little happiness, however incomplete.

"To do that one must be a diplomat, careful to be careful in one's judgments, to censure no one, to be considerate of all men while showing favor to none. What these men do when they are not here is their affair. But of this matter today, words will be exchanged. I will not have this sort of things happening in my place. I will have nothing to do with it."

"I was more or less expecting it. Especially here, although it often happens to a stranger in a strange town."

"I'm sorry it happened. For a cause, senor, I could die, if need be. But I have no cause. I am a neutral who prefers to remain so. Nor can I die for nothing, and to tell you of anyone here would be to die for nothing. I abhor waste."

"They told me you were the boss of Apple Valley?"

"Things are not always what they seem, senor. I *was* boss. There are changes taking place, changes not yet complete."

"I see I must talk to the man on the cliff. I'll ask him what he wants with Kilkenny, and why he wants me alive . . . rather than dead."

"Kilkenny?" She took a half step forward, incredulous. *"You?"*

"I am Kilkenny," he said.

"Long ago I heard of you. I heard many stories, but in most of them you were a good man. It was said that you fought only when absolutely necessary."

"I like it that way. I've tried to keep it that way."

"And you ride alone, Kilkenny?"

"Usually. Today Rusty Gates is with me, I think we have some interests in common."

"Are you never lonely, senor? For me it is sometimes so."

"Yes, it has been lonely," he said somberly. "It will be more so now."

Suddenly he saw her eyes widen a little, perhaps at something she saw in his. He took an involuntary step forward, and she seemed almost to lean to meet him, but he turned roughly away.

He had taken a stride toward the door when her voice caught at him. "No! Not now to the cliff, senor! The time is not now! There will be many guns! Trust me, senor, for there will be another time!" She stepped closer to him. "He alone will be enough for you . . .

even for you, Kilkenny, without the others. And he hates you!

"Why, I do not know, but he hates you! He is evil, senor, a fiend! He will not rest until he kills you, but he would do it himself, and slowly, with malice.

"Go now, and quickly! He will not shoot you if you ride away. He wishes to face you, senor. He wishes to see you die, to watch you die, and he wishes you to look upon his face, knowing it was he who killed you! This has been said, senor!"

Kilkenny was watching her, listening rather to her tone than her words, and now he turned half to the door. Then he looked back.

"Nita, I will do as you suggest. I will ride away. I do not know why you wish it, and it may be that you are protecting the man you love. But I do not believe that.

"I will go because I trust you, and trust your judgment. It may be that a man who trusts a woman is one who writes his name upon water, but this time I shall take the chance."

He went through the door to the street and Rusty followed. Lance untied the bridle reins and stepped into the saddle.

The doors opened and Nita Riordan stood there, looking at him.

"Who are you?" she asked, almost despairingly. "*What* are you?"

"I am Kilkenny," he said quietly, "only Kilkenny. No more than that."

He walked his horse down the street and out of town without looking back, and Rusty Gates rode with him, somewhat behind, as if to cover his back.

When they were safely out of town, Rusty rode up beside Lance. "I don't know what you did, Mister," he said grimly, "but you sure started something back there! I never saw Nita Riordan as she was today! She's always mighty cool, almost never smiles, never gives an inch on anything.

"A lot of men have made their move and most of them got a jolt. She hoss-whipped a couple, knifed one, and Jaime Brigo killed a couple. But mostly they just ride in and look, then ride away talking to themselves."

"Never put trust in a woman's emotions, Rusty. Or read anything into them. Every woman has her own way of showing what she is, and this one is no different."

"We just talked, that's all. No doubt she is lonely. I have been lonely also, and she sensed that, and then she did not want me killed . . . That's all there was, so don't imagine more."

Behind them, in the saloon at Apple Valley, one of the doors at the end of the bar opened and a man stood framed there. He was a large man, powerfully built with a dark, Indian, strangely handsome face. He was a big man, larger even than the bartender.

He moved down the bar with no more sound than that of wind along the floor, and he stopped close to Big Ed, who was now more calm.

"No," Brigo spoke softly. "You will not betray the senorita!" His black eyes were dark with intent as they looked into those of Big Ed Gardner. "If one word of what was said here reaches *him*, you will die. Not easily, amigo mío, not easily at all!

"There was the fight, then they talked quietly, those two together, the red-haired one and the man Kilkenny, and then they left. Do you comprehend, senor?"

"I ain't talkin'," Ed said irritably. "I got enough trouble! When I'm feelin' better I'm goin' to clear out! *Out!* Do you hear?"

"I hear . . . But wherever you go, you will say nothing of this, or I will follow and find you. I have followed others, senor, for less."

"Forget it!" Ed shook his head. "I'm quittin'."

CHAPTER X

Nita was standing in her garden, one hand idly fingering a rose, when Brigo came through the hedge. His lips parted over perfect teeth.

"You have found him, senorita," he murmured, "I can see that. You have found this man for whom you have waited."

"Yes, Jaime, I have found him. But has he found me?"

"Did you not see his face? His eyes? *Sí*, senorita, Jaime thinks he found you, too. He is a strong man, that one. Perhaps," he canted his head, "as strong as Brigo!"

"But what of *him?*" Nita protested. "He will kill Kilkenny. He hates him!"

"*Sí*, he hates. But I do not think he will kill. I think something new has come. This man, this Kilkenny, he is not like anyone else." Brigo paused. "I think soon, senorita, my work will be done, and I shall return to my home. I think that now he will do my work, this Kilkenny."

"What can we do, Brigo?"

"Nothing now, senorita. We must wait, and watch while we wait. But do not forget, senorita, this man is not the same. This Kilkenny, he is different, I think."

Trailing a few yards behind Kilkenny, Rusty stared up at the wall of the valley. A ragged, tree-clad slope fell away from the rim. It was a wild, lonely country, and he began to see that what Kilkenny suspected was probably the truth: someone planned to bring off the most colossal rustling plot in western history.

With this corner of the Live Oak country under one brand, cattle could be eased across its range and poured through the mouth of the funnel into Mexico. By weeding the larger herds carefully, they might bleed them for years without anyone discovering what was taking place. On ranges where cattle were numbered in the thousands, a few head from each ranch would scarcely be missed. But in the aggregate it would be an enormous number.

This was not a sudden plan of the moment. This was no foolhardy scheme devised by a puncher needing a few dollars for a binge in town. This was stealing on a grand scale. It was the plan of a man with a brain and ruthless courage. Remembering the three men killed in the street, Rusty understood that the "boss" would kill without hesitation and on any scale.

Kilkenny, as he rode, was doing his own thinking. The man who was directing the action was someone who knew him. Carefully, Lance began to sift through his memory for some hint as to who he might be.

Dale Shafter? No . . . Shafter was dead, killed in a fight stemming from the Sutton-Taylor feud. Anyway, he was not big enough for this.

Card Benton? Too small, a mere small-time rustler and gambler.

One by one Lance sifted their names, and man after man cropped up in his thoughts, but few living men had reason to hate him. And although a few had reason enough to fear, they were not the kind to conceive this sort of plan, nor act as this man was acting.

Who had fired upon him the night in the hollow as he waited for Mort? Who had killed Sam Carter?

Was it the same man? Or had the killings been done by such as the three who had attempted to take him in the Border Bar?

Try as he might he could find no man who fitted the picture he had, and the more Lance thought the more he wondered if it were only a simple rustling scheme. Yet what more could it be?

This job of helping Mort Davis, of saving his place, was developing into something far greater. Yet one thing he had done. He had proved to himself that neither Steele nor Lord was involved.

Men who were deadly with guns were as much a part of the west as Indians or buffalo. It stood to reason that when all men used guns, some would be better than others. And they were both, good and bad, essential to the building of the west. Kilkenny was one of the few who understood his rightful place in the western lands. He knew what he was and what he stood for.

Billy the Kid, Pat Garrett, Wes Hardin, Bill Hickok, Earp, Masterson, Tilghman, John Selman, Dallas Stoudenmire, Bill Longley and Pink Higgins . . . all were gunfighters. They belonged to the rough outer bark of the spreading westward tree.

Many of the gunfighters became marshals of western towns. No matter how lawless they themselves might have been, they became a force for order who kept anyone from disturbing the peace, bothering citizens or interfering with business.

Yet the man upon the cliff was different. He held himself aloof. He might have been one of the others, but one who had somehow changed his pattern and his style.

Shadows grew longer as they moved. A light breeze, picked up from the south, brought the scents of Mexico. There was a faint smell of dust in the air. Kilkenny glanced at Gates.

"Somebody fogged it along this trail," Kilkenny commented, "and not very long ago."

Rusty agreed. "Means no good for us," he said. After a moment he added, "Wonder what his next move will be?"

"Seems likely they'll try to bust things wide open between Lord and Steele before we can get them stopped," Kilkenny said. "It's all they can do."

"The worst of it is," Gates grumbled. "We've no idea what they'll do or try next."

For a long time they did not talk, each busy with his own thoughts and the need to be alert. Yet they saw no movements, heard no sounds. Several times they saw antelope, and once a deer. They startled a coyote gnawing on an old bone, a coyote that fled into the brush at their approach, but slunk about to await their passing.

They found a place to camp, backed against a low red cliff. There was a good field of vision on all sides except the cliff, which prevented all approach on that side of the camp.

While gathering wood, they placed a few slabs of rock in place to better their position if attacked. Then they built a small fire and made coffee.

"You goin' back there?" Rusty asked, after awhile. "To see Nita Riordan?"

"Could be." Kilkenny added a stick to the fire. "She's quite a woman." He paused again. "Whoever's atop that bluff seems to have everybody scared."

"You look at the three men he shot? Everyone of them shot through the skull, and he was shootin' from a good four, five hundred yards!"

"He might have found a closer position," Kilkenny suggested, "but let's figure he can shoot. He's somebody with enough reputation to scare some pretty tough men. I don't think Nita Riordan is scared, but she's wary. This man threatens her whole existence."

"Odd she'd stay there anyway. That's a handsome woman, and she seems well off. I mean, she owns that place, her house, some mighty fine horse-flesh and they say she has cattle on the range in Texas."

"No accounting for folks," Kilkenny said. "Some like it here, some there. I've seen some happy people in some of the worst dumps of creation. It seems to me she's a woman who makes her own world and isn't much influenced by what others think or do."

They watched the coals turn to a deeper red, then finished the last of the coffee. "You think we should keep watch? They'll be huntin' us."

"Leave it to Buck. He's pure mustang and we've

traveled together a few years now. He'll warn us in time."

At daybreak Kilkenny rolled from his bed, shook a scorpion from his boot and tugged it on, then the other. Meanwhile, his eyes were busy.

The buckskin was cropping grass, unalarmed, which would not be the case if anyone were in the vicinity.

They were in the saddle, riding toward Botalla at a good gait when they saw a rider winging it toward them. Rusty waved him down.

"Hey, what's the rush?"

"All hell's busted loose!" the rider shouted. "Lord's hay was set afire, and a Steele fence was cut in three, four places. Some Lord an' Steele men had a runnin' fight, and there's been two gun battles in Botalla!"

"Anybody killed?" Kilkenny asked.

"Not yet, far's I know. Two men wounded on Steele's side. If you boys ain't itchin' to fight, you'd better ride clear of Botalla. The lid's goin' to blow off!"

"Take it easy," Kilkenny suggested. "A little shooting needn't mean a war."

But the cowboy had slapped spurs to his horse and was gone, leaving a cloud of dust trailing behind.

"Looks like we're too late," Rusty said. "What'll we do now?"

"Stop it, if we can," Kilkenny said, "and if we can't, keep after the man who started it."

It was dark before they reached Botalla, riding by devious routes. There were lights in the Spur, and more lights in the larger Trail House. Kilkenny swung down, took the thongs from his guns and went into the Trail House.

Men turned quickly at the sound of his boot heels on the walk, and the jingle of his spurs. Their voices died down when they saw him, and they waited, watching him.

"Any Steele men here?"

Two men stepped forward, wary, expectant and ready for anything. Neither was a gunfighter. Both were simply tough, hardworking cowhands, but loyal to the brand.

"We ride for Steele," one said. "What about it?"

"My advice is, go home. There'll be no war. You stay away from Lord men, do you hear?"

A puncher with a scarred face said, "You mean if I get shot at, I don't shoot back? You must be funnin'."

"They cut our fences," the other man protested.

"Did they? Or did somebody else? Did you boys set Lord's hay afire?"

"No! I'll be damned if we did! I think he set it afire himself, just for a reason to have at us."

"Stop and think and you'll know that's not true. Lord wouldn't burn a whisp of his hay for any one of you boys. You're being pushed into a fight by somebody else."

"Yeah?" The scarred puncher was skeptical. "Who?"

"When I know that," Kilkenny said quietly, "I'll talk to him. In the meanwhile, let's not get excited and push this into a shooting war nobody wants, where nobody can win."

The scarred puncher shrugged. "I punch cows," he said, "I'm no gunfighter. If you can stop the fightin', more power to you."

Kilkenny turned and crossed to the Spur. Shoving through the door he told the Lord men what he had told the Steele men. Several of the men appeared relieved, but one man got up from a table and walked slowly across the room toward Kilkenny.

Lance Kilkenny knew what was coming. He had seen it many times before, in many places. He had seen it happen to him and to a dozen others, known for their ability with guns.

He knew the type. This man was undoubtedly fairly good with a gun. He was a man with a local reputation on his ranch or in the town he came from, and he wanted a reputation like Kilkenny's. Yet even as Lance watched the man coming toward him, he could sense his uncertainty. He was doing this because he believed it was expected of him, by himself or others.

He was coming now, but he was unsure. Kilkenny had the confidence of tested skill, and of many victories.

"You, Kilkenny! You swing a wide loop, tellin' people when to shoot an' when not to! It's time somebody called your hand."

His hand was poised over his gun butt but he froze into immobility. Kilkenny's gun was already in his hand.

In the few gun battles the man had been in, it had never happened like that. There had been a moment of tenseness and then both men reached for their guns. This had not been that way at all. The man had spoken. And then he was looking into a gun muzzle and that tall green-eyed man was behind it.

It came to him with a shock that all he had to do to die was drop his right hand, and all at once he very much wanted to live.

He had seen men gut-shot before, and suddenly he knew he did not want to die. He did not even want to be a gunfighter. He was a cowpuncher and a good one.

He took a slow, careful step back. "Mister, I reckon I just took in too much territory. I don't think you'll have trouble with the Steele boys tonight."

"Thanks," Kilkenny replied. "There's too much trouble on this range as it is."

Lance turned on his heel and walked from the barroom.

The man turned to the others. "Did *you* see him drag that iron? I thought I was fast, but—"

"Fellers," the scarred puncher said, "I think we better look closer. Kilkenny could have shot Jimmy, and he didn't. He may not be on our side, but he surely ain't on theirs. Let's just back off an' take another look."

Outside, Rusty Gates stopped Kilkenny. "There's a man rode in today, stranger around here, and he asked for you. Says he has something you need to know. He's from El Paso."

"El Paso? Who'd want to see me from there?"

Gates shrugged. "The man was pretty well liquored up, they say. But he's not talkin' fight, just that he has some news for you. Mighty important news."

"El Paso . . ," Kilkenny frowned thoughtfully. He had not been in El Paso since the Weber fight. Who could wish to see him from there?

"Where is he now?"

"Over at the Trail House. He came in right after you left. Tall, rangy galoot, looks like a cowhand. I mean, he doesn't size up like no gunman."

They stepped down off the walk and started across the street and had taken no more than three steps when they heard the hard report of a gun in the Trail House.

One shot, and then another.

Gates broke into a run but hesitated at the door. Kilkenny came up to him, pushed the door open with his left hand and stepped in quickly. Gates followed and moved to the right of the door.

A man lay sprawled on the floor, lying on his face, a red stain growing on the back of his shirt. A drawn gun lay near his hand. He was obviously dead.

Bert Polti stood just beyond the man, a gun still in his hand. As their eyes met, Kilkenny could see the instant calculation in Polti's eyes.

Was this the time? Kilkenny knew what Polti was thinking, how he was estimating the situation. He had a gun in his hand and Kilkenny had not. But there was Gates, off to one side and out of line. Kilkenny saw the impulse born, saw it die.

Polti was no fool, so he was doubly dangerous.

"Personal fight, Kilkenny," Polti said. "Nothing to do with the cattle war. He knocked a drink from my hand. I suggested he apologize. He told me to go to thunder and I beat him to the draw."

Kilkenny's eyes went past Polti to a puncher from the Lord ranch.

"That right?"

"Yeah," the puncher said, his face expressionless. "That's about what happened."

Polti hesitated just a moment, then holstered his weapon and walked outside.

CHAPTER XI

Several men moved toward the body, and Kilkenny looked down at the man. As they turned him over, he shook his head. The man was nobody he had ever seen before.

Then Rusty told him what he had already guessed. "That's the man who was looking for you," he whispered. "Seems mighty odd that he'd get himself killed right now."

Kilkenny's eyes caught those of the puncher who had corroborated Polti's story, and with an almost imperceptible move of his head, Lance brought him to the bar.

"If you will, you might tell me just what happened."

The puncher looked around, obviously uncomfortable. "Ain't healthy to shoot off your face around here," he muttered. "You see what happened to that gent?"

"You don't look like a man who'd scare easy," Kilkenny said. "All I want is the truth. Are you afraid of Polti?"

"No. I ain't afraid of him or you either. It just ain't healthy to talk. An' that Polti an' his outfit, they have spies ever'where. Howsoever, what Polti said was true. Though it did look to me like Polti deliberately bumped that cowboy's elbow, then pushed him into a fight the puncher didn't want."

"That puncher now," Rusty said. "What had he been sayin'?"

"Nothing to rile Polti, that I could see. He was

sayin' he had a story to tell you that would bust this country wide open. He was drinkin' pretty good and he was talkin' more than was good for him no matter what he was saying, and just a lot of folks were listening."

"Anything more?"

"Just more of the same. You know how it is with drunks, they get to harpin' on one subject and they repeat themselves."

"Did he say who he was? Or if anyone sent him?"

"No, not that I heard."

Bert Polti then, had deliberately picked a quarrel with this man who had a message for Kilkenny, and had shot him down before the message could be delivered.

What was it the man had said or known that might be dangerous to Polti and his group? And why from El Paso?

Suddenly a thought occurred to Lance.

Finishing his drink, he said out of the corner of his mouth, "Stick around and keep your eyes open, Rusty. If you can, keep an eye on Polti."

Leaving the Trail House, Kilkenny walked slowly down the street, keeping to the shadows. Crossing the alley to the hardware store, he walked along beside it, then past the corral until he reached the hotel.

No one stood or sat on the porch, so he stepped up on the porch and went through the door like a ghost. All was quiet and still. The small lobby was empty but for the glassy eyes of the elk and the buffalo who stared down at him with threatening gaze.

The old man who acted as desk clerk was lying on the leather settee, snoring softly. Sam Duval, the owner, sat in a big leather chair, a newspaper opened across his lap and partly on the floor. He, too, was asleep.

Kilkenny turned the register around. It was a gamble, and only a gamble.

It was the fifth name from the top: *Jack B. Tyson, El Paso, Texas.*

Room 22.

Kilkenny went up the stairs, swiftly and silently.

There was no sound in the hall above, for those who wished to sleep were already snoring, and those who wanted bright lights and red liquor were still in the Trail House, the Spur and other such establishments along the street.

Somewhere in his own past, Kilkenny felt sure, lay the secret of the man on the cliff above Apple Valley, and this strange rider from El Paso might have been bringing him that very information, or perhaps some clue to what was happening here.

There are few secrets, and they remain secrets but a very short time. What someone knows, someone will repeat, always warning the other party to say nothing. But that party also has a wish to impart information, and it is invariably passed on again.

Also, for any criminal venture such as this one seemed to be, it was necessary to recruit men, and not all the men approached would agree to the terms. So somebody always knew something, and such word passes from saloon to saloon, from hide-out to hide-out.

Perhaps . . . and it was only a chance . . . something in Jack B. Tyson's war-bag might be a clue, some clue to the why of his killing. It was unlikely that the authorities, such as they were, would have searched his room yet.

There was every chance that Polti might have, however.

Of one thing Kilkenny was certain. The killing of Tyson—if that was indeed his name—had been deliberate.

The hallway was dark, and Lance felt his way with feet and hands. When safely away from the stairhead he struck a match. The room nearest him was number 14.

A few steps farther, his fingers touched the door and traced the numbers: 22.

Gently, he turned the knob. Like a ghost he slid into the room, but even as he stepped in he saw a dark figure rise from bending over something at the foot of the bed.

There was a stab of flame in the darkness, and something sent a hot iron along his ribs, then the figure leaped through the open window, rolled down the shed roof and jumped off that roof to the ground.

Kilkenny stepped to the window and snapped off a quick shot at the man as he disappeared. Even as he fired, he knew that he had missed.

For an instant he considered giving chase, but then he dismissed the idea. The man would be mingling with those in the Spur or Trail House, or down the street at one of the cantinas.

There was the pounding of running feet on the steps and in the hall. Removing the lamp globe, Lance struck a match and lit the lamp.

The door slammed open and the clerk stood there. Behind him, clutching a shotgun, was Sam Duval.

"Here! What the consarn are you doin' in here? Who fired those shots?"

"Take it easy, Dad," Kilkenny said, smiling. "I came up here to have a look at Tyson's gear and caught some thief going through it. He shot at me."

"What rights have you yourself, comin' up here?"

"Jack B. Tyson was killed a short time ago in the Trail House. He had been looking for me, said he had something for me. So I came to get it. Also, I'll have to take charge of his gear and arrange for his burial."

"Well," Duval grumbled, "I guess he ain't in no condition to object, and I did hear him say he had word for Kilkenny. All right! Go ahead an' put his stuff together. He done paid when he come in, so's he don't owe nothing. But no more shootin', you hear? Folks have a hard enough time sleepin' as it is."

He turned and stumped down the narrow stairs, following the clerk.

Alone in the room, Kilkenny began a painstaking examination of the dead man's gear. Jack Tyson had brought little with him, and what he had brought was typical of a wondering cowhand, offering no clue to anything.

Nor was it much to leave behind. A couple of blankets and a ground-sheet, a yellow slicker, a broadcloth coat with four extra cartridges in one pocket, some matches and a letter, months old, from a girl.

He had found no clue, and whatever Tyson had planned to tell him was lost forever now, buried in the dead man's skull, as Polti had intended.

Lance had hoped for a quick solution to the problems, but there was no solution here. Nor had there been any settlement of the range difficulties. If he could just get Davis, Steele and Lord together! The three were cut from the same cloth and would be friends, given a chance. Davis's only trouble was that he had come into this part of the country too late.

The introduction of wire had sparked this fire, and would do so at other places as well, yet the crux of the problem was not barbed wire.

El Paso . . . What was there in El Paso that tied in with this?

What had he forgotten?

Lance's warnings and arguments might have averted a major clash tonight, but the range war was still coming and he was little closer to heading it off.

Whatever was intended was being neatly arranged by someone with an eye for detail, and someone who knew the area. Had Mort Davis not sent for him, the chances were that things would have gone forward without a hitch.

The fact that the mysterious figure behind the scenes seemed to hate Lance Kilkenny was beside the point, yet it had now become a major factor in the plans.

What of the Brockmans? They were in the area, supposedly somehow involved. But there was nothing Kilkenny could be sure of.

For a long time he had been sure that one day he would kill the Brockmans, for it was certain their paths would cross, and the Brockmans were aggressive, fearless trouble-makers. Kilkenny did not like trouble-makers. And especially he did not like those who used their strength to tyrannize others, as the Brockmans did . . .

Suddenly Kilkenny froze.

An idea was coming into his mind, all uncalled for. An idea that might change everything.

CHAPTER XII

Bert Polti *might* have killed Wilkins and Carter, but Lance had no hard evidence.

Again and again his thoughts returned to the house on the cliff and the feeling that he must go there. He was not foolish enough to believe he could do it without risk, for he must go alone, and there were too many imponderables, too many intangibles, too many unknown things that he could not foresee.

Lord and Steele might postpone their fighting for a day or two. It might even come about that they wouldn't fight, yet the problem of Lost Valley would remain. And the man at Apple Canyon would try to force the issue at any moment.

Standing in the dimly lit hotel room, Kilkenny let his gaze drift about him. There was nothing. Obviously the man had entered the room, combed his hair and then gone out for a drink. Lance was starting to leave when the memory came to him.

The man who had fired at him before, the man who had killed Carter, had stopped on the spot to reload.

A careful man, obviously. But then, a smart man with a gun was always careful.

Kilkenny searched the room again, knowing even as he did so the search was useless.

Then he went down to examine the ground where the man had fallen, or dropped. He found two deep indentations where the man had landed . . . on his feet.

The tracks were plain enough and Kilkenny followed them, holding a match to the ground here and there, occasionally catching a glimpse of a toe or heel mark in the light from a window.

Sixty feet beyond the hotel he found what he sought. The running man had dropped the shell of the spent cartridge, ejecting it from his pistol to reload. Kilkenny picked up the shell . . . the same type used by the man who shot Carter.

"Find somethin'?"

He straightened up, moving to one side as he did so. He had already recognized the voice.

It was Gates, standing there, his hand on his gun, facing him.

"A shell. Where's Polti?"

"Left for Apple Canyon, ridin' easy, takin' his time."

"You been on him as I suggested?"

"Yeah. If you're thinkin' that might have been him who did the shooting, forget it. I heard the shooting and then somebody came in and said you'd been playin' target down here. Polti was in sight all the time."

Kilkenny stared gloomily into the darkness. So it was not Polti . . . The theory that had half-formed in his mind that Polti himself was the unseen killer had to be discarded.

Suddenly he had a new thought. What about Rusty himself? What, after all, did he know about *him*? Why had Rusty joined him? From admiration, perhaps, or the sheer love of battle? Or for some deeper purpose?

He shook his head. If this continued, he would soon be suspecting himself. Turning, Gates at his side, Lance walked back to the hotel. He felt baffled, defeated. At whatever turn, he was outwitted.

The night was wearing on, and he was tired. Mounting the buckskin, he rode outside town. He had chosen a place some distance away. Tomorrow night it would be another place, which he would choose tonight.

To sleep in the same place on more than one occasion was a treat he rarely permitted himself.

Rusty had remained in town to keep an eye on what developed.

Lance lit no fire, but unsaddled Buck, led him to water, then let him roll before picketing him on some grass near the rocks, where he himself would sleep. The moon was rising and there was light enough . . . much more than he needed.

The moon was just clearing the ridge top when he heard a faint movement, the movement of somebody stirring around outside his camp.

Instantly Kilkenny rolled over behind a boulder, six-shooter in his hand.

Not fifty feet away, standing atop a small hummock, was the dark figure of a man.

"Don't shoot, Kilkenny." The soft drawl was pleasant to hear. "This is a friendly call."

"Come on in, but be careful. I can see just as well in the dark as in the light."

The man walked slowly, giving Kilkenny plenty of time to see him. He was obviously a man accustomed to dealing with gun-handy individuals. He stopped a dozen feet off.

"Sorry to come up on you thisaway, but I wanted a word in private and you're a right busy man these days."

Kilkenny waited. There was something vaguely familiar about the man. Somewhere, sometime, he'd seen him before.

"Kilkenny, you've the reputation of being a square-shooter. I need to know men like that. I'm Lee Hall."

Lee Hall! There wasn't anyone in Texas who had not heard the name of one of its most famous Texas Rangers. "Red" Hall, they called him, and he had tamed a few wild towns and a good many wilder men. All the Texas cow towns knew him, and along the border he was famous . . . and respected.

"Kilkenny, you've got a right to wonder why I'm here, but the truth is I need some information and I need some help. What's been happening down here?"

Briefly, Kilkenny sketched the events since his arrival, the message from Mort Davis that brought him here, and the shootings. He mentioned his efforts to quiet the cattle war and said a few things about his suspicions as to Apple Canyon.

"Nita Riordan? Never met her myself, but I think I knew her pappy. Came out here from Carolina or Virginny. A good man, an honest man, but impractical. Heard he had a daughter, but just never had occasion to ride into Apple Canyon myself."

"What do you want me to do?" Kilkenny asked.

"Keep on with what you're doing. The last thing we need is a cattle war. I'm putting wire on my own place now, and we've having troubles, too. If you need any help, just send word. But consider yourself sworn in. You're a deputy now."

They walked over and sat down together against the rock wall. "Funny thing, this mention of the killings of Carter and Wilkins. They aren't the first who were killed in this neck of the woods. For the past six years there have been unexplained killings. Chet Lord's half-brother was dry-gulched . . . and not far from Apple Canyon. Name of Destry King. Never did find out who did it and there wasn't anything we could tie on to. Yet only a few days before he was killed Destry told me he thought he knew who was going to do it."

For two hours they talked, keeping their voices low. Much of the talk was speculation.

"Can't move in without some evidence," Hall said, finally. "And no way to prove these shootings have any connection with the others, but I've a hunch you should fight shy of Nita Riordan . . . She's trouble. I don't mean personally, but trouble happens where she is, and I don't like the look of it. Sometimes I think something's going on down here that's out of my field . . . away out."

Destry King? Kilkenny remembered the name from somewhere, but not here.

"What about Nita Riordan?" Kilkenny asked.

Hall shrugged. "Nothing against her but the company she keeps. In our books she's clean as a whistle. Brigo's killed a couple of men but I've no doubt they needed it. There's a story that her pa once did something for Brigo or his family. Don't quote me, as I only heard the story second-hand and it probably wasn't right, but somebody told me that Brigo promised her father he'd see her safe and married before he returned to his own people.

"So far as anybody can see he's a man totally without interests except for her. He seems to consider himself her uncle or something of the sort, but whatever you do, steer clear of him. He's hell on wheels with any kind of a weapon."

Long after Lee Hall rode away into the darkness, Kilkenny lay awake, puzzling over the little he knew.

Using his saddle for a pillow, he stared up at the stars, turning over all the persons involved, and all the problems. The knowledge that there had been earlier killings was more information that refused to fit any theory he evolved of what was going on.

Could it be there was something else happening here that had begun long ago? Something that had nothing at all to do with cattle, rustling or barbed-wire on the range?

Destry King, half-brother to Chet Lord, had been killed when he thought he knew who the killer was going to be. Had he confided in Chet Lord? Or Steve?

It was high time he had a talk with Lord, as he had with Steele. Circumstances had conspired to keep him busy, but now he would make the time. His messages until now had been sent through Steve.

He slept then, and a low wind whispered through the clumps of oak, moaned softly around the rocky ledges, and the coyotes called plaintively to the lonely moon.

It was night, a soft, beautiful night, a night of moonlight. And then the slow dawn came and the buckskin nudged him awake.

CHAPTER XIII

Lance Kilkenny headed out for the Cottonwood before the sun was up. At the small station he sent three messages, one to El Paso, another to Dodge, and the third to a friend in San Antonio who had long lived in the Live Oak country, but who had grown up in Missouri.

Leaving Cottonwood, he cut across country to the Apple Canyon trail and rode for the Chet Lord ranch. He was cutting through a narrow defile when he glimpsed two people riding toward him. They were Tana Steele and Victor Bonham.

"Howdy," he said cheerfully. "Nice day."

Tana reined in and faced him. "Hello. Are you as insulting today as ever?"

Lance chuckled. "Do you mean am I still as stubborn about spoiled girls as ever?" He grinned. "Bonham, this girl is sure a wildcat, but she's a pretty one."

Bonham laughed, but his eyes went to the tied-down guns and when they lifted there was a strange expression in them. Bonham reined his horse around, broadside to Kilkenny.

"Going far?" he asked politely.

"Not far."

"Chet Lord's, I suppose. I hear he's an unpleasant man with whom to do business."

"I suppose we all have our moments. We'll get along, I think. I can do business with most men, pleasant or otherwise."

"Aren't you the man who killed the Weber brothers?" Bonham asked. "I heard you were. I should think it would bother you."

"Bother me? I never think of it. I wasn't hunting trouble. They were. It doesn't worry me much, one way or the other."

"I wasn't thinking of conscience," Bonham said. "I was thinking of Royal Barnes. I have heard he was a relative of theirs, and one of the fastest men in the country."

"Barnes? I never gave him a thought. The Webers asked for it and they got it. Why should it bother Barnes? I've never seen the man, and wouldn't know him if I did."

"He might not like his relatives being killed. And he's said to be very fast . . ."

Kilkenny ignored the easterner, not liking the tone of his voice. For there was something pushing about it, something prying that he did not like.

He turned to Tana who was watching him, a curious light in her eyes.

"Ma'am? Did you know Destry King?"

"Destry King?" Her eyes came alive. "Oh, yes! We all knew Des! He was Chet Lord's half-brother. Stepbrother, rather, for they had different parents. He was a grand fellow. I had quite a crush on him when I was fourteen."

"Killed, wasn't he?"

"Murdered. Someone shot him from behind some rocks. Oh, it was awful! The killer walked up and shot him twice in the stomach, and then in the face."

Bonham sat listening, but his eyes on Kilkenny were puzzled.

"I don't believe I understand. I thought you were averting a cattle war, but now you seem curious about an outdated killing."

"He was killed from ambush, Bonham. So were Sam Carter and Joe Wilkins. So were several others. The murders do cover quite a period of time, but none of the killings was ever solved, and it looks a bit odd."

Bonham's eyes were keen. "I see. You feel there may be a connection? And that the same man may have killed them all? That some of these killings had nothing to do with the cattle war?"

"I think the present killings are part of the range war," Kilkenny said, "but the style of the killings is like those old crimes." He turned back to Tana. "Tell me about Des King."

"I don't know why I shouldn't," she said. "Des was a wonderful fellow. Everyone liked him, and that's what made his murder so strange. He was a very good man with a gun, and one of the best riders and ropers around.' Everyone made a lot of Des, but he was a very regular fellow in spite of it.

"There had been several riders killed, and then an old miner, but I think the first one was an Indian. He was an old Comanche, harmless enough, who used to live around the Lord ranch.

"Altogether I think there were seven men killed before Des started to investigate. He had an idea that all seven were killed by the same man. He even warned me once that I shouldn't go riding. He said it was no longer safe for anyone to ride alone . . . All the victims had been alone at the time."

"You rode a good deal as a youngster?"

"Oh, yes! There weren't many children around and I used to ride over and talk to Steve Lord. Our fathers were good friends then, but it was six miles of rough country to their ranch . . . very wild country."

"Thanks," said Lance. "I'll be getting on. Much obliged for the information, ma'am. Glad to have seen you again, Bonham."

Bonham smiled. "We'll probably see each other often, Kilkenny."

Suddenly Tana put out her hand.

"Really, Kilkenny, I am sorry about that first day. I knew you were right the first time, but I was so mad I hated to admit it. I'm sorry."

"Think nothing of it. But I'm not going to take back what I said about you."

Tana stiffened. "What do you mean?"

"Mean?" Lance's eyebrows lifted innocently. "Didn't I say you were mighty pretty?" He touched a spur lightly to the buckskin's flanks and was gone.

After a brisk gallop of a quarter of a mile he slowed down, busy with his thoughts.

Hall's information had been correct, and Des King had indeed had a theory about the identity of his killer. No doubt such a man would have been tracking him down, putting together one item with another and drawing hourly closer. And then the killer, realizing he would soon be exposed, had killed King.

But what was the thread that connected the crimes? None of the bodies had been robbed.

Yet where was the connection, except in the manner of the killings? And why had the pattern varied in the case of King, who had been shot several times, shot as if the killer carried a particular hate for him?

Why a harmless old Indian? A prospector? And several riders?

Just ahead of him, the ground dipped into a wide and shallow valley following a cattle trail over which stock had recently been driven. Nearby was a wash, and a pile of rocks just beyond.

Kilkenny glanced at both, taking in all the approaches to the rocks with a glance that missed nothing. He pushed his hat back on his head, looked toward the arroyo and shifted his Winchester a little. He did not believe an ambush awaited him, but he was prepared.

So far the Steele-Lord fight was hanging fire. Either his suggestions had struck home or some other factor was in operation. Twice there had been minor bursts of action, but for the present all seemed quiet. Yet the basic trouble remained, and Mort Davis had not been brought together with Lord and Steele.

North of the Live Oak the country was seething, too. Wire-cutters had been busy, and there had been sporadic fighting. Cattle had disappeared occasionally, but in small bunches, and there was no evidence that they had come down through the Live Oak country to the border.

Kilkenny had almost reached the Lord ranch house when he saw Steve riding toward him. Steve threw him a quick, careful look, his eyes curious, but friendly.

"Didn't expect to see you over here. I thought you were headed for Apple Canyon."

"Apple Canyon? Why?"

"Oh, most people who meet Nita Riordan once want to see her again. Are you looking for Pa?"

"That's right. Is he around?"

"Uh-huh. That's him on the roan horse."

Together they rode up to the big man. Kilkenny was pleased. Chet Lord was a typical cattleman of the old school. Old Chet turned and eyed Kilkenny as he approached, looking quickly from him to Steve.

He smiled and held out his hand.

"Kilkenny, is it? I figured so from the stories I been hearin'."

Lord's face was deeply lined, and there were creases of worry about his eyes. Either the impending cattle war was bothering Chet Lord, or something else was. He looked anything but a healthy man now, yet it was not a physical distress. Something, Kilkenny felt instinctively, was troubling the rancher.

"Been meaning to ride over, Mr. Lord," Kilkenny said. "I've got to keep you and Steele off each other's backs, then get the two of you together with Mort Davis."

"You might get me an Webb together, but I'll have no truck with that cow-stealin' Davis!"

"Shucks," Kilkenny grinned. "You mean to tell me you never rustled a cow? You never slapped a brand on some critter with a doubtful ancestry? I don't think there's a cowman in Texas who hasn't been a bit free with an iron now and again."

Lord chuckled a little. "Well . . . maybe. But that Davis came in here and settled on the best piece of grazing in the country!"

"What did you expect him to do? Pick the worst? What kind of a man do you want for a neighbor? Mort's an old buffalo hunter. He was in this country while you were still away back in Missouri."

"Maybe. But we used this range first."

"How'd you happen to come here, anyway? Didn't you like Missouri?" asked Kilkenny.

Chet Lord slapped a hard hand on his pommel and glared. "That's none of your damn business! I come here because I damn well felt like it, an' for no other reason!"

His tone was sharp and irritated, and Kilkenny detected a sign that the man was very near the breaking point. But why? What was riding him? What was the trouble?

Kilkenny waved a casual hand. "I'm sorry, Lord. I meant nothing. Only you and Steele have been damn hard on Davis, and he's a man you'd like if you just got acquainted." He paused. "By the way, what's your theory on the killing of Des King?"

For a moment Kilkenny thought the older man would have a heart attack. His face went shockingly white and he clutched hard at the saddle horn. Lord's teeth set and he turned his tortured, frightened eyes at Kilkenny.

"You better git!" Lord said, after a minute. "You better git goin' now. An' if you'll take a tip from a man, you'll keep movin'! You hear?"

He turned his horse and walked him away. Kilkenny puzzled, watched him go. Then feeling eyes upon him, he turned to find Steve Lord staring at him, that strange, white look to his eyes that Kilkenny had glimpsed once before.

"Don't bother Pa," Steve said. "He hasn't been well lately. He's not been sleepin' good, and I think this range war has him worried."

"Worried?"

"Uh-huh. We need money, Kilkenny. If we lose many cows, or this war ruins our range, we'll not be able to pay our debts. He's a good man, Pa is. Too good a man, I think. Don't worry him no more, Kilkenny."

They talked quietly then, of range conditions, of vanishing cattle and of the trouble between Steele and Lord.

After a few minutes of this, Kilkenny rode his buckskin away from the ranch. Something about Des King was bothering Chet Lord. Well, why not? The man was his brother. They had been raised together, even though King had been much the younger man.

Was Chet himself the killer? No. Kilkenny could not accept that. There was no coyote in Chet Lord. He might kill a man in a stand-up fight, but he'd never shoot one in the back.

Yet, when he thought about it, Kilkenny had a strange feeling that Chet Lord had been worried about Lance Kilkenny, and not about himself.

Was it a preminition of some kind? Why should Chet Lord worry about Lance Kilkenny?

Why should anybody?

What weird, strange thing was happening here, that drove such a man as Chet Lord to the verge of collapse?

CHAPTER XIV

More and more the chain of events grew tangled. Kilkenny could sense powerful forces building up about him, and nothing so tangible as a simple gun battle awaited him.

Death rode the dry trails of Texas, and the border was now a haunted place where no man knew what tomorrow might bring.

Danger Kilkenny had always known. It was a way of life along the border and in the western lands. It was a thing one accepted with the rising and setting of the sun, and one dealt with it as best one could.

The long dry miles without water, the blazing sun, the cold blast of wintry winds, the rush of the stampede, the howl of wolves, the bucking of a wild horse

. . . these were but taken in stride. *And* the settling of disputes by gun. It was a way of life—and a price one paid for the freedom, the space, the opportunity.

Yet what rode here was fear. A haunting thing, an elusive enemy that none could see, but one that struck suddenly from the silences.

Kilkenny was used to guns. Forced into a gun battle at sixteen, he had killed his first man.

Since then he had lived with an awareness of death, as had these other men around him. The wild lands offered much to live for but many ways in which to die, none of them easy. It was something a man accepted.

Steve Lord had implied that there was financial trouble, yet remembering the fat cattle he had seen, and the range over which he had ridden, Kilkenny could not convince himself that was true.

It was a cover-up for something else. There had been fresh paint on the Lord buildings—all too rare in Texas—new ranch buildings and new barbed wire.

Yet on the range a killer was loose, a fiendish killer who could kill ruthlessly and without warning. Somewhere in all this welter of trouble and trial there had to be a clue to who he was.

Kilkenny lifted his head and stared down the shadowy valley before him. He was riding back the way he had come, something he rarely did, and which he had scarcely noticed until now, so busy had he been with his thoughts. He glanced ahead, and the old instincts came alive. He was suddenly uneasy.

"Lord's instilling his fear into me," he muttered, half-aloud. "A man's a fool, though, to ride back over the same trail."

The buckskin was suddenly restive, tossing his head and snorting.

What he did then was sheer impulse. He whipped his horse around suddenly and took it in two quick jumps for the shelter of the wash.

As the buckskin gathered himself for the second jump, Kilkenny felt the *whip* of a bullet past his face! Then another and yet another, but the buckskin was running all out now and Kilkenny was weaving among the scattered oaks and cedars.

Buck knew what bullets were, and when he hit the edge of the wash he slid to the bottom, legs braced, and in the bottom, he wheeled and raced down the wash at top speed.

Right before them the bend took a turn, and if Buck could make that bend they might out-flank the killer.

Lance went around the bend at a dead run, drew up sharply and hit the ground, Winchester in hand, running all out. Flattening himself behind a hummock of sand and sagebrush, he peered through. He moved, trying to see better and a bullet kicked sand into his eyes. He slid back into the wash.

"Spotted me, damn him!"

He sprang to the saddle and circled farther, then again tried the bank. Now he could see the nest of rock from which the killer had first fired.

Nobody was in sight. Then he caught a flicker of movement higher on the hill.

The killer was stalking *him!*

Crouching low, Lance watched a gap in the rocks. When he caught a shadow there, only a blob of darkness from where he huddled, he fired.

It was only a snap shot, quick, offhand, and it clipped the boulder, ricocheting off into the fading light, whining wickedly.

Then it began, a deadly game of chess, with each man holding a rifle, each maneuvering for a killing shot. Twice Kilkenny almost nailed him, and once a shot clipped a leaf within an inch of his skull.

An hour passed, and Lance had seen nothing. He kept turning, listening, watching the buckskin. Then he began the deadly game of stalking once again, working higher and higher up in the rocks.

Then he found it. A place where a man had knelt to fire, on the ground was a cartridge shell from a Winchester '73.

He picked it up. "Now that might help," he mused. "Not too many of them around. Most of the Rangers have them, and I've got one. Rusty still uses that old Sharps.

"But say! Tana had one, and if I'm not mistaken, Bonham was packing one."

Three times now the killer had fired at him, if all three shots had been fired by the same man. Bonham was in the vicinity, but what reason could *he* have?

Actually, it might be one of many people, all within the general proximity of the places where the firing was done.

Kilkenny was no nearer discovering the killer now that in the beginning, although he had shells from the killer's six-gun as well as his rifle. Yet he had no evidence aside from a healthy hunch that all the shooting had been done by the same man.

Did the mysterious boss at Apple Canyon have anything to do with it. He had not wanted Kilkenny killed then, so why now?

Bert Polti could be ruled out. Who else had reason to want him dead?

There seemed to be no real reason behind any of the odd killings that had taken place. Some strange influence seemed to be at work, something cruel and evil, something untypical of the range country where men settled their disputes face to face.

Kilkenny avoided trails and worked his way cross-country, varying his route constantly until he reached Botalla. The important thing now was to get Steele, Lord and Davis together to settle their differences. Knowing all three, he was sure they could reach an agreement.

The two big cattlemen were range-hungry, and Davis was a stubborn man, accustomed to making his own way, fighting his own battles, and asking favors from no man. Each was a rugged man, accustomed to driving ahead. But now they must learn that much was also to be gained through cooperation and mutual assistance.

Botalla lay quiet under a late sun when the buckskin walked down the street. There were the usual loafers sitting around, the usual rigs along the street, people buying supplies or engaged in other business in the town and the locality. Among them were several punchers from the Lord and Steele outfits.

Kilkenny drew up alongside two of them. A short cowboy in bat-wing chaps and a battered gray hat looked at him from his seat on the boardwalk, rolled his quid in his jaws and spat.

"How's things?" he asked, warily.

"So, so," Kilkenny shoved his hat back on his head and wiped the sweat from his brow. "You're Shorty Lewis, aren't you?"

The short puncher looked surprised. "Sure am. How'd you know me?"

"Saw you one time in Austin. Ridin' a white-legged roan."

"I'll be damned! You sure got a memory. Indians stole that hoss off me three years back. You sure saw me, all right."

"Got to have a memory, living like I do. A man might forget the wrong face." He stepped down from the saddle. "You ride for Steele, Shorty?"

"Six years. Before that I was up in the Nation."

"Did you know Des King?"

Lewis got up slowly. "What's on your mind, Kilkenny? Des was half-brother to Lord, but he was my friend. We rode together up in the Nation."

"Lewis, I've been doing some nosing around, and I've got a hunch that the same man killed Des that killed Carter and Wilkins and a few others around here."

"But King was killed years ago!" Shorty protested. "Long before this fight got started."

"Right. I think somebody is riding this range with some other reason for killing men. There's a man loose . . . man or woman . . . who is utterly cold-blooded and vicious. He may have some reason we don't know, but I think he's killing for the love of killing. Trouble is, he'd liable to blow the lid off this cauldron and have a lot of good men on both sides shooting each other."

"What kind of a man would that be? Maybe you've

got something there, for why would a man shoot into Des after he was down and helpless? Somebody who stood right over him? I was one of the ones who found the body, and Des was alive and struggling when those last shots were fired into him."

Shorty Lewis looked thoughtful.

"The way he'd moved around in the dirt made us think he'd been paralysed by the first shot, and that then the killer had walked up and deliberately gut-shot him whilst looking right straight at him."

"There was an Indian killed before that, and a prospector, too. Did you know them?" asked Kilkenny.

"Sure . . . Everybody knew them. Old Yellow Hoss was a Comanche. He done a favor for Lord some time back and the old man kept him around . . . sort of on a pension-like. He was a good old boy, no harm in him, although in his day he'd been a heap big warrior. Well, one day we found him out on the range, shot in the back.

"No reason for it we could see, and the same with that old prospector . . . I forget his name, now. The prospector's stuff had been gone over but nothin' missin' but a bone-handled scalpin' knife he used to pack around. He had no enemies anybody could think of, and nothin' worth stealin'. His rifle wasn't taken, and his hoss an' burros were left adrift."

"Where were they killed?" asked Lance.

"Funny thing there. All were killed betwixt Apple Canyon and Lost Creek Valley. All but one. Des was killed on Lord range not far from Lost Creek."

"Shorty? How about you askin' Chet to come in tomorrow for a peace talk? I'll have Steele and Davis there."

Shorty Lewis agreed.

After telling some of the Steele hands to ask Webb to come in, Kilkenny walked his horse down to the general store. Old Joe Frame was selling a bill of goods to Mort Davis's son. Through him, Lance sent word to Mort.

Rusty Gates was lounging on the boardwalk in front of the Trail House.

"If you swing a loop over the three of them it'll go a long way in the direction of makin' peace in the Live Oak. At least this piece of it."

"Yes," Kilkenny said, "after we find who is doing all the killing, and round up that outfit at Apple Canyon."

Gates nodded. He touched his tongue to the edge of the cigarette paper and deftly rolled his smoke.

"May not be so hard. You've been makin' friends, partner. Lots of the local people have been talking to me. Frame, Winston, Doc Clyde, Tom Hollins, and others. They all want peace, and they want some law in Botalla. They intend to show up at your peace conference, and they say if you need a posse, they'll be ready."

"That's good news, the best news. They should carry some weight with both Lord and Steele."

"Think they'll try to break up your peace meeting?"

"They might, at that, but I've been thinking and I've got a little plan. . . ."

Morning sunlight bathed the dusty street when the riders came in from the Steele ranch. Webb was in the lead, riding with Tana, Jim Weston and two Steele riders. One of them was Shorty Lewis.

Rusty and Kilkenny were standing in front of the Trail House when they rode in. "She's sure pretty," Rusty said, staring at Tana. "Prettier'n a button."

"Why not marry the gal?" said Lance. "Old Webb needs a bright, cow-wise son-in-law, and Tana's quite a girl. She's a mite spoiled, but a good steady hand on the bridle and she'd hold her gait."

"Marry *her?*" Rusty shook his head. "You must be out of your mind. She wouldn't even look at the likes of me. Anyway, I thought you were fixing to put your brand on her."

"Not me," said Lance. "Tana's all right, but a man with my reputation had better stay clear of women. Marriage isn't for me, Rusty, although there's nothing I'd like better than a place of my own and the right woman. But sooner or later I'll be too slow on the draw and she'd be a widow.

"No, I've been riding alone for a long time now, and I'll not break any woman's heart by getting myself killed. Right now there's nobody. I'm a man alone."

Lance paused. "If I was to change, it wouldn't be Tana. I like to tease her a little, because she's had it too easy with men and everything else, but that's all. If I ever find a woman to tie to, she'll have to be one with staying quality, the kind who can ride where I go, live as I live, and stay right with me through it all.

"It would be no life for a woman, Rusty. There's loneliness and change and moving all the time, roosting no place, and always the chance of a shot in the back by somebody hunting a reputation, or some brother or friend of a man who took cards in the game and drew too slow at the finish."

Webb Steele had rounded his horse to the hitching rail and swung down. Kilkenny looked at him with amused appreciation. Webb rode like a king, dismounted like one, and walked into the Trail House as one who commands, whose rights have never been questioned.

There were many such, and they had not come to it at once, for men who walked that way had won the right to do so. They knew what they could do and they did it.

A few minutes later, Chet Lord came in with Steve. Then the door opened and Mort Davis stood there. He stared bleakly at Steele and Lord, then crossed to the fireplace and stood with his back to it, his thumbs hooked in his belt, prepared for whatever might come.

Kilkenny sat down at the head of the table. "Guess we should call this meeting to order, gentlemen," he said, quietly. "The way I hear it Lord and Steele are disputing about who fences in Lost Creek, and Mort here is holding Lost Creek."

"He's holdin' it," Steele said, "but he's got no right to it."

"Easy now," Davis said imperturbable. "How'd you

get your range, Steele? You just rode in an' squatted. Well, that's what I done. I'd been figurin' on settlin' Lost Creek for fifteen years. I come west with Jack Halloran's wagon train and saw Lost Creek then."

"Huh?" Webb Steele turned sharply around. "You rode with Halloran? Why, Tana's mother was Jack Halloran's sister!"

Davis stared at him. "You're not foolin'? You all from Jackson County?"

"We sure are! Why, you old coot! Why didn't you tell me you was *that* Davis? Jack used to tell us how you an' him—"

Webb stopped suddenly, looking embarrassed.

"Go right ahead, Steele," Kilkenny said, smiling. "I always knew if I could get you two together you'd be friends. Same thing with Lord here. You're all good men. Each one of you has a good outfit and you can build it into something better.

"You, Steele, are importing some fine stock. So is Lord. Mort doesn't have the money for that but he does have Lost Creek and he's got a few head of cattle and the start of a herd. I don't see why Lost Creek should be fenced. Fence out the upper Live Oak country if you like, but you three can get along and work well together.

"Somebody has moved into Apple Canyon and organized a bunch of rustlers. They've got to be cleared out, lock, stock an' barrel. I'm taking on that job myself."

"We need some law here," Steele declared. "How about you becoming marshal?"

"No," Kilkenny looked around at their faces. "Lee Hall dropped by my camp the other night, and deputized me, so I'm already an officer of the State of Texas.

"Before I ride out of this country I've got two things to do. I'm going to clean up Apple Canyon and I'm going to get the man who has been doing those killings."

His eyes touched Chet Lord's and the big rancher's face was ashen.

Steve Lord spoke suddenly. "You make that sound as if you believed there's no connection between those shootings and the cattle war."

"There may be no connection. That remains to be discovered. But I think the person who killed Wilkins and Carter is the same person who killed Des King and the others. I think we have an ugly, vicious murderer loose on the range, and I intend to find him.

"And when I find him," Lance added quietly, "he'll hang!"

CHAPTER XV

Chet Lord slumped in his chair, looking old and tired.

Tana Steele had an odd look in her eyes, her cheeks pale and drawn.

"I think," Kilkenny said, "that Des King knew who the killer was. He was killed partly to keep him from exposing the killer but in part because the killer hated him."

"If he knew who the killer was," Steve protested, "why didn't he tell anyone?"

Kilkenny looked up at Steve, smiling slightly. "Maybe he did," he said slowly. "Maybe he actually did."

"What do you mean by that?" Webb Steele demanded. "If he told anybody, I never heard of it!"

Tana's face was tense, and Chet Lord closed his eyes tiredly, and said nothing. Steve glanced at his father, his own face stiff and hard.

"Des," Kilkenny said slowly, "had him a little hangout in a box canyon west of Apple Canyon, and he kept a diary, an account of his search for the killer. He had an idea there might be an effort to kill him, so he dropped a line to tell Lee Hall, and Lee told me. Tomorrow I'm going to that cabin in the canyon and get that diary, if Lee hasn't already got it. Then we'll have the whole story."

"I think—" Tana got up abruptly, but whatever she was about to say was lost in a burst of gunfire, a wild yell from the street and then a roll of heavy firing.

Kilkenny left his chair with a lunge and kicked the door open. There was a burst of firing just as he emerged and started down the steps. His foot caught on a broken step and he fell headlong, his head striking a rock lying at the foot of the steps.

Rusty and the others rushed after him and were just in time to see two big men running for their horses, while rifles and pistols began to bark from all over town.

One of the big men threw up his pistol and blazed away at the group on the porch. Rusty had just the time to grab Tana and thrust her to the floor, as bullets spattered the hotel wall.

Kilkenny, his head throbbing from the fall, crawled blindly to his feet with the instinctive drive of the fighting man to continue the battle.

There was a pound of charging hoofs, then horses charged by him. One caught him a glancing blow with its shoulder and he was again knocked flat. Another rattle of gunfire, and it was over.

Kilkenny got to his feet, wiping the dust from his eyes. There was a trickle of blood from a slight cut where his head had hit the rock.

"What was it? What happened?"

Old Joe Frame came running along the street from the general store carrying an old Sharps buffalo gun.

"The Brockmans! That's who it was! Come to bust up your meetin' and wipe you out! Jim Weston, Shorty and the other Steele rider tried to stop 'em."

Webb Steele came down the steps, gun in hand, eyes hot with anger. "Damn' near killed Tana! Boy," he grabbed Rusty by the shoulder, "you've got a head on you! Saved her life! You can ride for me any time! Anytime at all!"

"Weston's hurt bad," Joe Frame said, "and Lewis is hurt. The other boy—O'Connor, his name is—he's shot up. By now he may be gone. O'Connor never had a chance. He dropped his hand for his gun and Cain Brockman drilled him dead center. The boy was still alive . . . I don't know how he did it.

"Abel took Lewis and they both lowered guns on Jim Weston. It was short and bloody, but I don't think either one got a scratch."

"This time they've gone too far!" Steele shouted angrily. "We'll go out there to Apple Canyon and burn 'em out!"

Tana Steele, white-faced and shocked, got up shakily, helped by Rusty. "You saved my life!" She pointed at the wall behind her, where now there was a spattered line of bullctholcs. "I would have been killed!"

Kilkenny saw blood on Rusty's shirt. "You'd better take him inside, Tana. He's been shot."

"Oh!" Tana gasped. "You're hurt!"

"It ain't nothin'! Shucks, I—" He slumped against the wall.

Helped by Steele and Frame, Tana got Rusty Gates inside, and strctchcd him out on a sofa.

Kilkenny watched them go, then turned, as behind him he heard a board creak.

It was Bert Polti. "All right, Mr. Lance Kilkenny, here's where you cash in your chips!"

Polti had a gun in his hand, and the gun flamed as Kilkenny turned. Lance felt the hot breath of the bullet, and then he fired.

Polti staggered, but caught himself. His head thrust forward sharply and his teeth bared in a kind of ugly snarl. He wanted desperately to get off another shot but his gun wouldn't come up.

He tried. Bracing his feet he took both hands and attempted to lift the gun, but slowly lowered the muzzle, he took a staggering step and fell, all in one piece.

Steele came charging to the door, gun in hand. He took one look, then holstered his gun.

"Polti, is it? He's had it comin' for a long time."

Steele looked thoughtfully at Kilkenny. "Polti was a bad one. You must be just as good as they say."

"Steele," Kilkenny said, "you and Lord get your men and stand by. I'm going after the Brockmans myself, and when I come back we're going to clean up Apple Canyon. Right now, the Brockmans come first."

"You're going after them alone?"

"I am. If you'll see that Rusty is cared for."

Steele chuckled. "Tana's doin' that. He's quite a man, that Gates is."

A half hour later, with a three-day supply of grub, Kilkenny hit the trail. For the first half mile the Brockmans had ridden hard, Then they had slowed down to save their horses, when they noticed no pursuit. They were shrewd riders and they could save their horses by confusing their trail.

Three miles out, they took to the rough country, crossing an outcropping of rock, weaving through clusters of boulders and around clumps of oak brush and trees.

They used every trick of wilderness men to hide their trail, and they were as good at it as any Apache. The trouble was that the man behind them was better. Nonetheless, it slowed him down.

Soon it was evident that the Brockmans were traveling in a wide circle. Picturing the country in his mind, Kilkenny decided they were headed for Cottonwood.

Buy why Cottonwood?

Could they by chance know of the wires he had sent? Were they afraid of what the answers might mean to them? Or were they watching the station on orders from the man in the cliff house?

On impulse, Kilkenny turned from the trail and cut right across country to the railroad line. Few rails were down yet, but the road had been surveyed, materials had been dropped along the route and work was beginning. Keeping to every bit of cover he could find, Kilkenny headed cross-country for the lonely station.

That night he bedded down on the same creek that flowed through Cottonwood, about six miles upstream from the village. He lit no fire, contenting himself with chewing on a piece of jerked beef and drinking from the stream.

At daylight he checked his guns. He knew the Brockmans and was under no misapprehension as to their abilities. They were good alone and almost unbeatable together.

If only by some trick, some stratagem, he could get them one at a time!

It was a good thought, but the two Brockmans ate together, worked together, slept together.

It was almost nine o'clock when Kilkenny rode into Cottonwood, and if his calculations were correct he was still ahead of the Brockmans.

Reaching the tiny cluster of huts, he tied the buckskin under some trees at the edge of the stream, then crossed the log foot-bridge to the street—if such it could be called.

There was nothing much to Cottonwood. At one side was the small stream, never more than six feet wide, and some cottonwoods and willows that lined its banks.

There was the station with its telegraph office—built ahead of the rails for the convenience of the surveyors —a saloon and general store, then four or five houses. That was all.

Kilkenny walked into the station.

"I'm Lance Kilkenny. Any messages for me?"

The station-keeper nodded. "Yea... Just come in. Three of 'em. I didn't know who you was."

He handed the messages to Kilkenny, broke a straw from the broom and began to chew reflectively, glancing out of the window from time to time.

"Be some fireworks now," he commented, indicating the messages. "It sure beats the devil."

Kilkenny had pocketed the messages without reading them. After glancing into the saloon, he crossed the street to the willows. On the other side of the bridge, in a little hollow among the trees, he stretched out and began to doze.

An hour later the stationmaster called out loud
enough to awaken him:

"Hossmen comin' out of the breaks, Kilkenny. Look
powerful like them Brockmans!"

Kilkenny got up, yawned and stretched. Then, leaning against a huge old cottonwood, he waited.

CHAPTER XVI

The riders turned into the road leading to Cottonwood at a fast trot. There were three of them now. Kilkenny did not know the third man.

They drew up suddenly in front of the bar and
two of the riders swung down. Kilkenny noted with
appreciation the way they glanced along the street, then
looked across at the station.

Kilkenny walked across the bridge.

Abel Brockman heard his footsteps on the bridge
and glanced over his shoulder. His body stiffened and
he said something, low-voiced, and started to turn.
The Brockmans had been caught offside.

Up the street a man sitting on a bench before the
store fell backward off a bench and scrambled to get
under cover. Cain Brockman was still in the saddle,
but he grabbed for his gun. His horse, startled, veered
sharply. As Abel's hand moved, Kilkenny's hand
dropped in the draw for which he was famous. As
Abel Brockman's gun cleared the holster, Kilkenny
fired.

Walking toward them he opened up with his right-
hand gun, firing each time his right foot hit the ground.
Abel got off a fast shot but Kilkenny's bullet had
knocked him staggering and the shot went wild. Abel
stumbled into the hitching-rail, grabbed for support

with his left hand and Cain's horse reared wildly, something Buck would never have done.

The big man, raising his own gun to fire, all his attention on Kilkenny, lost balance and fell from the saddle. Kilkenny walked on, firing.

Abel sank to one knee, then came up shooting.

Unbelieving, Kilkenny stopped, steadied his hand and fired again. He was sure he had hit Abel with at least four shots.

Abel, falling, lost his grip on his gun. Kilkenny swung to get a shot at the third man but he, grabbing Cain Brockman, dragged him around the corner out of sight. One of the horses trotted after them.

Kilkenny, gun in hand, walked up to Abel. Lying on his back in the dust, hand clutching an empty gun and his chest covered with blood, Abel Brockman stared up at him.

"Damn you! Cain will kill you for this! Cain'll . . . *Oh!*" His face twisted with agony. "Cain . . . where's—"

One hand lifted up, straining, and Kilkenny, who had looked toward the corner, heard the pounding of hoofs. He started to run. Rounding the corner he saw the third man, whoever he was riding away, holding Cain Brockman before him on the saddle, riding off up the trail.

For a moment Kilkenny stared after them, gun in hand. Then he holstered the gun and walked slowly back. He did not believe he had hit Cain Brockman, but the big man had been thrown hard and had hit the ground hard. A concussion, no doubt.

Kilkenny retrieved Buck and stepped into the saddle. As he passed the station, the stationmaster leaned out. "Didn't think you could do it, mister! Some shootin'!"

"Thanks . . . And thanks for the warning." He indicated the dead man. "Better get him out of the street. He's a big man and he'll spoil mighty fast."

He started Buck toward the Botalla trail. Whatever was going to happen would happen fast now, and he had crossed part of one of the roughest hurdles.

He slapped Buck on the shoulder and lifted his voice in song.

> *I have a word to speak, boys,*
> *only one to say,*
> *Don't never be no cow-thief, don't*
> *never ride no stray.*
> *Be careful of your rope, boys,*
> *and keep it on the tree,*
> *But suit yourself about it, for it's*
> *nothing at all to me!*

Even as he sang, one part of his mind was reaching forward to the problems that lay ahead. It was time to strike. Now, before any further move was made by the man at Apple Canyon. If he and the men from the ranches could roust out the rustlers living in the long house there, and either capture or send them across the border, much of the trouble would be ended.

Polti was dead and Abel Brockman was dead . . .

They must move now. At once.

When Cain Brockman came around, he would come hunting him—of that Kilkenny had no doubt. And despite the death of his brother, or because of it, Cain was a very dangerous man.

Yet Kilkenny was almost positive in his own mind that the man at Apple Canyon and the mysterious killer were not the same.

They might be . . . but they seemed to Kilkenny to be vastly different types. The latter would kill only for reason and most of that reason would be gain, while the other person, man or woman, seemed to kill for no reason at all . . . except in the case of Des King.

On a sudden hunch Kilkenny turned the buckskin and took off across the hills toward Apple Canyon. Another talk with Nita might give him some clue, some indication of who the man on the hill was.

Or was he simply fooling himself? Was it not that he wanted to see her again? Yet what right had he to think seriously of any woman?

He rode on, his face somber, thinking of her. A man

who rode the outlaw trail had no right to think of any woman. There were many who did not feel as he did, and that was all right for them. But Lance Kilkenny had seen too many good women and some bad ones, left alone after gun battles. He had taken the news to a few of them himself.

What did he have to offer? Nothing. No life beyond the day, no future, no trade or profession beyond the cattle business.

And someday his gun would hang in its holster, his elbow would bump something, or somebody would grab him at the wrong moment. Confident as he was of his skill, Kilkenny knew that someday he would be too slow.

Yet there had been a few gunfighters who had left it behind. A few . . . very few . . . but some had. One had become a lawyer, another a newspaper man.

Men who lived by the gun died by the gun, and that was the usual way of it. So far, Lance had been lucky because he was elusive. Those reputation-hungry kids did not know who he was and, once they found out, he was gone. For he never stayed where he had had a gun battle. Nor would he remain here, once the trouble was over. He would ride out, disappear.

The buckskin skirted the base of a hill and emerged among some cedars. Below him lay Apple Canyon.

Kilkenny studied the town, and there was no telltale flash from the cliff house. He might be able to get into the town without being seen. Keeping to the cover of the scattered trees, he worked his way down the slope. There was no sign of life.

At the foot of the hill he dismounted and tied the buckskin with a slipknot. Enough of a tie to tell the buckskin he should stand, not enough to hold him if Kilkenny should whistle. Keeping the saloon between himself and the livery stable, Kilkenny walked casually from the trees toward the back of the saloon.

The biggest chance of being seen was from the Sadler house, or by someone walking that short street. Yet Kilkenny made the trees near Nita's house without being seen, far as he could tell.

Placing a hand on the fence, he vaulted it, landing lightly behind some flowering shrubs. Inside the house, someone was singing in a contralto voice, singing lightly and without pretense—as people sing when the song comes from the heart and not the brain. It was an old song, a tender song, and for a moment Kilkenny stood listening, strangely moved by the beauty of it. Moving around the shrubbery he stood by an open window.

Nita Riordan stood inside, almost within reach. She held an open book in her hands. She was not reading, but looking out at the hills across the valley, a wistful expression around her mouth.

"A lovely picture," Lance said gently. "A very lovely picture! It makes me wish I were a painter, that I might capture and hold it forever!"

She did not jump or show surprise, but turned to face him.

"It is strange that you should come just now, for I was thinking of you. I was wondering what you were like as a little boy, what your mother was like, and your father."

Kilkenny removed his hat and leaned on the sill. "Does it matter? No man is anything but what he makes of himself, I suspect, although no doubt the inheritance is there. It is what he does with what he was given that matters, and I have not done so well."

"I would not agree. You are an honorable man, a brave man, and a man with pride, But no foolish pride. I think that is quite a lot."

"I've killed men."

"That is the way of the world, I'm afraid. We live in a time when quarrels are settled in such a way, and when many men must enforce their own law. A time will come when that is no longer necessary, I hope."

He shook his head. "Nita, there have been times when I knew trouble was coming and did not avoid it. Sometimes I have stood at a bar and seen a man whom I knew meant trouble walk into a room. I should have left at once, and I did not.

"You have power when you can use a gun, but it is an ugly power. And it worries me that someday I might kill the wrong man."

"Kilkenny, I am young, yet not so young as most women who are married. I am twenty-four, and have kept a saloon for several years. In that time I have learned much about men.

"This is a violent time. But if only bad men could use guns the world would be in a sorry state. We need such men as you, men who know when to use and when not to use guns, men who will carry them not as a threat but as a protection for themselves and others.

"What would I have done without Brigo? How could I have lived? I inherited this place. It was all I had, and I knew no other way of making a living.

"I have done well . . . very well . . . but without Brigo I would not have lasted. Men know he is here. Men know he is remorseless. Men know what he would do if harm should come to me. So I have been safe."

"You are a smart girl, Nita. And shrewd enough to know what the end will be for me."

"I do not know any man's end. Who knows what his life will be? Who knows how long he has to live? Do you? Do I? Does Brigo?"

"You have been thinking a lot, Nita."

"Perhaps too much. It is what comes of living much alone with books. I am not sure whether in these days a girl should think . . . or, at least, whether she should let a man know it."

"I wouldn't have a girl who didn't think. Beauty is much, but it is not enough. I'd want a companion . . . if I could think at all of such things."

"You have thought of it."

"Maybe . . . But look what I have to do now. He is up there, and I must find him. Once and for all this trouble must be ended."

"Be careful, Kilkenny. He is deadly. He is as vicious as a coiled snake, and he lives now for just one thing: to kill you. Once, when he was drinking he told me he knew he could beat Hardin or Longley, and there were but two men who bothered him. You and Ben Thompson.

"He said Ben Thompson had more nerve than any man he'd ever known, and if you ever fought him you'd have to be sure he was dead, because as long as he could walk he'd come after you again.

"You bothered him because you were like a ghost. Here, then gone. Nobody could tell him anything about you except that you were powerfully good with a gun."

"I know how it is," said Lance. "You're good with a gun and you begin hearing about others, and after awhile you start to wonder whether they are better than you and what would happen if you met. You form a picture in your mind of what a man is like, and when you shoot that picture is in your mind. When you know nothing about a man, it worries you.

"When a stranger rides into town, say a quiet man who drinks with his left hand, well, you know he might be dangerous, but you don't know who he is. Once you know, you understand what you're up against . . ."

They stood there for a few minutes without talking, and a strange yearning arose within Kilkenny. It was the longing of a lonely man for a home, a fireside, for the nearness of a woman and the laughter of children. For someone to work for, to protect, someone to belong to, and some place where you fitted in.

There had been so many years of endless watchfulness, of continual awareness, of looking into each man's eyes wondering if he was a man you would have to kill, or if he was the man who would have to kill you.

Yet even as he thought of that, Kilkenny knew there was something in his blood that answered to the wild call of the wilderness trails. There was something about riding into a strange town, swinging down from his horse and entering a strange saloon, something that gave him a lift, that gave a strange zest to life.

There was something in the pounding of guns, the feel of a .45 in his fist, the power of a horse beneath him and the shouts of men that awakened all that was free within him.

Times bred the men they needed, and the west needed men who could bring peace to the wild land— even while finding death for themselves. The west was won by gunfighters no less than by pioneering families and Indian fighters.

"And when this is over, Kilkenny, what will you do?"

"Ride on. Maybe I'll find myself a place in the hills and change my name and just live away from trouble."

"Why don't you marry and have a home, Kilkenny?"

"Me?" he laughed harshly. "All I can do is handle a gun. That isn't much good around the house. Of course, I might punch cows or play poker."

He straightened suddenly. "Time I was getting on. You be careful."

He turned away, then asked, "Nita, what hold does this man have over you?"

"None. As I told you, I wish to live, and he would kill a woman as quickly as a man. But, after a fashion, he too has protected me. Of course, he wants me for himself, and one of the things that has protected me is that he is perfectly sure he will have me. But I belong to no man . . . not yet."

"You can't tell me who he is?"

"No. Perhaps you think I do not help, but if he kills you I shall again be alone, and he will be here, and I must live. I can tell you but one thing. Do not go to his place by the path."

Kilkenny walked back to the buckskin and rode back to Botalla. If the men were still there he would ride back at once. He had scouted all the approaches to Apple Canyon.

He believed he could muster sixty men, and that was not enough, for there were at least forty at Apple Canyon, and they would be defending their home grounds.

Nevertheless, nothing could be gained by waiting and much might be lost. The time was now.

Yet the raid on Apple Canyon might still leave the killer at large. As Kilkenny rode, his brain sifted the accumulated evidence, little though it was. Yet one idea refused to be denied, and it worried itself around in his thoughts until he arrived in Botalla.

He came up to the Trail House at a spanking trot.

Dropping from the saddle he flipped a dollar to a Mexican boy. "Pedro, take this horse and treat him right—oats, hay and water . . . and a rubdown."

Pedro grinned. "*Sí*, senor. It shall be done."

Rusty Gates was inside the Trail House, holding himself stiff, but he was there, and he had a gun belted on.

"If you're goin' after the Brockmans, count me in."

"Abel's dead. Cain had a bad fall and was knocked out."

"When he comes out of it, he'll go crazy. He'll be after you."

"Can't help it. We're riding to Apple Canyon."

"Might be sixty, seventy men there," Joe Frame said, "but we're ready."

There was a pound of hoofs in the street, and then a man burst in the door. "Kilkenny! Chet Lord's dyin' an' he wants to see you!"

"What happened?"

"Gored by a mad steer. Hasn't got long, but he keeps askin' for you."

"Steele, if you will, get the men together. Lots of ammunition and grub for three days. Post guards so nobody slips out of town to warn Apple Canyon. Start whenever you're ready, and I'll catch up!"

The Mexican boy was busy with the rubdown. Together they saddled and bridled the buckskin.

Riding to the Lord ranch, Lance wondered what it was that was on Chet's mind. That something *was* on his mind was obvious. The man had lost weight, he was drawn and pale, and it was obvious his nerves were on edge.

Was Chet Lord the unknown killer? As soon as the idea came to him, Lance put it aside. The man was not the type. Bluff, outspoken and direct, he was a man who would shoot straight and die hard, but all his shots would be at a man's face, not his back.

Letting the buckskin have his head, he hurried along the road. The buckskin knew his master well, and knew he would be called upon for many hard rides. He was ready for them.

Although cow ponies were often held in slight esteem, most cowpunchers had their favorites. It was the gunmen and outlaws who cared for their horses, who worried over them, for a horse might spell the only difference between life and death.

Buck was as keenly sensitive to danger as any wild creature. A flicker of movement anywhere and he was instantly alert—which came of running wild in rough country.

The Lord ranch was strangely still when they came into the yard.

Steve met him at the door, his eyes filled with tears. His face was pale. "He wants you, Lance. He's been asking for you."

Kilkenny went into the room where Chet Lord lay dying. A sharp-eyed man with a beard straightened up as he entered.

"I'm Doc Wentlow." He smiled wryly. "From Apple Canyon. He wants to talk to you . . ." The doctor glanced at Steve, ". . . alone."

The doctor and Steve went out, and at the door Steve hesitated, as if loath to go. Then he went out and drew the door shut behind him.

Kilkenny turned to the old man on the bed. His breath was slow and heavy, but his eyes were open. His face seemed to have aged ten years, and when he reached out he grasped Kilkenny's hand with trembling fingers.

"Kilkenny," he whispered hoarsely, "I'm dyin'. Promise me you'll do it. It's something you can do."

"Sure. If it's anything I can do, I will."

"Kilkenny," he whispered, then his grip tightened on Kilkenny's hand. "Kilkenny, I want you to kill my son!"

"What?" Kilkenny shook his head. "You can't mean that."

"You've got to! I'm an old man, Kilkenny, and right or wrong, I love my boy. I love him like I loved his mother before him, but he's a killer! He's insane! Des told me before Steve killed him. Long ago Steve had a bad fall, maybe that done it. He acted queer after he began to straighten out, but I wouldn't believe it. He seemed to be all right, and then he started killing things. Animals . . . chickens. Finally he stopped that and seemed to have straightened out. Then the old Indian died, and others. I didn't see it, but Des did. I wouldn't believe Des when he told me, even though I could see it had to be true.

"Des said he'd have to be put away, but he was all I had, Kilkenny. I just wouldn't accept it.

"I done wrong. I know I done wrong, and folks died because of it. Sometimes he was a good boy. Thoughtful, kind . . . then he'd go to moonin' around and one day he'd ride off . . . An' somebody else would die.

"Kilkenny, you got to kill him. I won't be around to protect him no more, or to slow him down from his bad ways. You'll shoot him so he won't suffer. You're good with a gun, and you'd do it for a horse with a busted leg.

"I don't want him to suffer. He's a baby for pain. He can't suffer. I don't want him hung, neither.

"Just shoot him down. Kill him before he does more harm. Joe Frame has got a paper. It's all wrote down. I can't die knowin' I left an evil thing behind me to do more evil. An' but for that, he's been a good boy."

That was the last thing he said before closing his eyes. Of course, Kilkenny thought. It all fitted. The opportunity, the killing of Des . . . Everything. Kilkenny had even suspected something of the kind and that was why he had wired.

Wired?

Kilkenny clapped a hand to his chest. Why, the wires! He had forgotten, in the thought of the Brockmans coming, he had completely forgotten!

Hurriedly, he dug into his pocket and took them out. The first was from San Antonio and it was a verification of what Chet Lord had said, a few scattered facts about his fall. That information would be unnecessary now.

He unfolded the second message, from El Paso.

TYSON SAW ROYAL BARNES AT APPLE CANYON. HE KNEW BARNES FROM HAYS CITY. BARNES MURDERED TYSON'S BROTHER AND TYSON HEARD BARNES SWEAR

TO KILL YOU FOR KILLING THE WEBERS. BE CAREFUL, KILKENNY! HE'S COLD AS A SNAKE AND LIGHTNING-FAST!

Kilkenny crumpled the message and thrust it into his pocket. The third message no longer mattered. He had only tried to locate various gunfighters so he might decide who was at Apple Canyon, and now he knew.

Royal Barnes!

The name stood out boldly in his mind, for it was one he had long known. A man reputed to be boldly handsome, a cold, hard man, victorious in many gun battles, raids into Mexico, even raids against Indians. Some said, which Kilkenny doubted, that Wes Hardin had once backed down in front of Royal Barnes.

Kilkenny opened the door and stepped out. Instantly, Doc Wentlow got up.

"How is he?"

"Low," Kilkenny replied. "Where's Steve?"

"Steve? You know, he's acting strange. He stood by the door a minute, apparently listening, then he ran out, jumped on a horse and took off, riding like the devil!"

Kilkenny was relieved. He had never killed a man unless the man was attempting to kill him. To walk out and shoot Steve Lord dead would never have entered his mind. Just what he could do he was not yet sure, nor how to go about it. He did know that Steve Lord must be stopped.

Thinking back to that moment in the Trail House, he remembered the odd look in Steve's eyes that day, yet Steve had not wanted to shoot it out. His insane urge to kill might stem not from the fall but from some twisted sense of inferiority.

What Steve would *do* now, Kilkenny could not guess. He knew killers, but those he knew were, by and large, sane men whose ways could be understood. Even the craziest of men had moments of sanity, and were often good men, given the chance.

Now Steve had mounted and ridden away, to what? Where could he go?

Suddenly, Lance had an idea. Steve Lord would go to Apple Canyon.

However insane Steve might be, there was still some connection between him and Apple Canyon. Kilkenny suspected Steve had more than a little interest in Nita Riordan, but he would now be riding with fear in his heart, with the desperate realization that his last refuge . . . his father . . . was gone.

Now Steve was out in the open, a place he had desperately feared. He must fight, and he might die, and Kilkenny knew such a man would fight like a cornered rat . . . or simply fold up and not fight at all. Yet he, Kilkenny, had an obligation to a dying man, and he must do what he could . . . short of killing.

Why should he feel depressed? Steve was a killer, a man who had slain the innocent, who shot from ambush, and he *must* be stopped. His own father, the man who sired him, had passed the sentence upon him.

Kilkenny turned off into the brush, unrolled his poncho, and was asleep almost as soon as he hit the ground.

CHAPTER XVII

Botalla's main street was crowded with horsemen when Kilkenny rode back to town. They were in for the finish, these lean, hard-bitten, range-tried veterans of the Texas cattle country. Riders from the Steele and Lord ranches were there, men who had ridden the cattle trails north, men who had fought the Comanches and the Kiowas, men who were veterans of the War Between the States . . . on one side or the other.

Yet as Kilkenny rode up the street, his eyes searched for Steve Lord, and as he rode through the crowd he wondered how many of these men would be alive when the week had ended.

They would be facing men as tough as themselves, men reared in the same hard school, desperate as men

can only be when faced at last with the results of
their own misdeeds.

They would fight shrewdly and well, for they were
uncommon criminals, tough young men who for one
reason or another had found themselves on the wrong
side of the law. With a different turn of events, they
might be punching cows or trail-bossing herds.

Certainly, they would ask no quarter or give none.
A fight with them was a fight to the finish. They might
have taken the wrong trail but they had courage.

Kilkenny wanted none of that fight. He wanted but
one man: Royal Barnes.

How would he know him? Somehow, Kilkenny had
the feeling he would know Royal Barnes when he saw
him.

This meeting would be different, just as the fight
with the Brockmans was different. He had been for-
tunate in timing his meeting and his moves so Brockmans' combination would not work. He had killed
Abel Brockman without having to fight Cain, too.

That fight would come. Cain was around, and Cain
had announced his intention of killing Kilkenny.

Another thing he knew. He had never drawn
against a man as fast as Royal Barnes . . . with blinding
speed, exceptional accuracy, and a coldness Kilkenny, himself, did not have. Barnes had killed Blackie
Slade, and Kilkenny remembered Slade only too well.
He had seen Slade in action and the man had been
poison, pure unadulterated poison in a gun battle. Yet
according to reports, Barnes had shot him down like
he was an amateur.

He swung down from his horse and walked into
the Trail House.

"We're all set," Steele told him. "We've just been
waitin' to see what shape Lord is in."

"Chet Lord is dying," Kilkenny said, "and he told
me about the killings. Steve Lord has been dry-gulch-
ing those people. Des King uncovered it and told Lord,
but then Steve killed Des, and the old man just didn't
have the heart to take his own son up. But now Chet
Lord knows he's got to be stopped."

Steele shook his head sadly. "Too bad! But, we

should have known. Steve was always a strange one."

"There's something else, too. The man up in the cliff house that I was telling you about, the leader of all this trouble, is Royal Barnes."

In the stillness that followed, men stared at one another. And into the minds of each came the stories they had heard of the man, stories told in barrooms and around camp fires on the range. It was said that Royal Barnes had killed thirty men, but nobody knew for sure. Yet in the mind of each was the realization that he himself might be the next to go down.

Few killers had sought trouble. For the most part the gunfighters, while known to each other and with considerable mutual respect, had not hunted trouble. Royal Barnes had, both as a boy and as a man.

He had been a fairly good hand with cattle, but he had not worked at it. He had ridden shotgun for a stage line when he was seventeen . . . and killed two men who had tried to hold up his stage. Then he had hunted down the man who got away.

Only a few months later, Royal Barnes had received a tip that a holdup was to be attempted, so he followed the stage.

There were four men there, all in position, ready for the holdup.

Royal came up on them from behind and opened fire. One survived to tell the story. Afterwards, there were no more holdups when Royal Barnes rode the stage.

That had been the beginning. Then, for several months, he was marshal of a mining boom town in Nevada, and was reported to have killed two men. But from that time on, he seemed to have gone to the side of the lawless. It was reported, but unproven, that he had himself held up a stage in Montana. There had been several robberies on the trails of men who had struck it rich in the gold fields, and then Barnes had gone to Mexico.

He had been seen in Kansas City, had killed a gambler on a riverboat, had been in Abilene and then in Ellsworth. The next report had come from Leadville, where he had killed a man reputed to have been a minor member of the James gang.

Kilkenny was thinking fast of all these things when suddenly, the doors burst open. As one man, the men gathered in the Trail House turned to stare.

A full step inside the door, his big head thrust forward, stood a huge, broad-jawed, unshaven man in a checked shirt, black jeans, and heavy cowhide boots.

"Cain Brockman!" Old Joe Frame exclaimed.

Brockman walked toward Kilkenny and stopped, three paces from him. He unbuckled his gunbelt and put his guns on the bar. "I'm goin' to kill you, Kilkenny, with my bare hands!"

"Nothing doing!" Webb Steele said. "We've no time for that, Kilkenny! We've got a job to do!"

"The job will have to wait," Kilkenny said. "Cain has chosen his weapons. He'll have his chance."

With a hoarse grunt, Cain Brockman lunged, swinging a ponderous right fist. Kilkenny stepped inside with a left to the face, then closed with the bigger man, slamming both fists to his midriff. Cain grabbed Kilkenny and threw him bodily across the room into some tables and chairs, then lunged after him.

Kilkenny stepped away, stabbing a left that caught Brockman on the cheekbone. Then Brockman caught Kilkenny with a swinging right that knocked him to his knees.

A kick aimed at Kilkenny's head just grazed his shoulder as he was starting to rise. He lost his balance, toppling over on the floor. But as Cain rushed in to put the boots to him, Kilkenny rolled over quickly and came up swinging.

Brockman was savage, with a killing fury, and he was forty pounds the heavier man, with two inches of height and at least that much of reach. And he had before him the man who had killed his twin.

Another right caught Kilkenny a glancing blow, which he partially evaded. He went under a swinging left and countered with a wicked right to the ribs. He then hooked a left to the chin and sprang back before Cain could grab him.

It was toe-to-toe, slam-bang fighting then, with neither man taking precautions. They fought like savages. They stood wide-legged in the center of the floor and swung until it seemed impossible that they could continue. Then Kilkenny slipped under another left, and uppercut hard with both hands to the body.

The bigger man backed off and Kilkenny hit him with a long left that split his swollen cheekbone, showering him with blood. They grappled, and went to the floor, kicking and gouging.

Brockman was a brute for strength, and filled with so much hatred and fury that he was almost immune to pain.

There were no rules here, none of the niceties of combat. This was fighting to maim or to kill, and all the spectators knew it.

Blood streaming from a cut on his own cheek, Kilkenny lanced a left to Cain's mouth, missed a right and took a wicked left to the body. He took the punch going in, and landed both hands to the face.

Cain's head rocked with the force of the blows and he spat a tooth onto the floor. He swung hard to the head, staggering Kilkenny. But the gunfighter came back fast, ripping a short right uppercut to the chin, then a left and a right to the face.

Kilkenny was boxing now. Long ago he had worked with some of the best boxers of the day. He needed every bit of his skill.

It was not merely defeating Brockman. Kilkenny would soon be facing Royal Barnes as well, and his hands must be strong and ready. He stepped inside of a right and whipped a right to the heart, then hooked a left to the same place and battered away with both hands at the big man's torso, his head on Brockman's shoulder. Body punches had less chance of hurting his hands, and Kilkenny knew he must fight with care.

He stepped around, putting Brockman offside, then crossed a right to Cain's bleeding eye, circled farther and crossed the right again. He stabbed three fast lefts to the face and then, as Brockman lunged close, he butted him under the chin with his head.

Brockman let out a muffled roar and crowded Lance

to the bar, but Kilkenny wormed away and slugged the big man in the ribs.

Brockman seemed to be slowing down. His face was bloody and both eyes were swollen almost shut.

He backed slowly away from a stabbing left and was suddenly brought up hard against the wall. Putting a boot against the wall, he shot himself off it like a battering ram, head down, and caught Kilkenny in the chest. Off-balance, Kilkenny went to the floor.

Brockman rushed in, trying to kick him in the ribs, but Kilkenny got to hands and knees and hurled himself against Brockman's legs. The big man tumbled over him, and then spun around on the floor and grabbed Kilkenny's head, groping for his eyeballs with his thumbs.

Mad with pain and fear for his eyes, Kilkenny tore loose and scrambled to his feet. Brockman came up swiftly and Kilkenny jabbed with a left to that wide, granite-hard face. Blood flew and he felt the nose crunch under the blow.

Cain crowded in, seemingly impervious to pain, pounding at Kilkenny's midsection, but Kilkenny blocked swiftly, catching most of the blows on his arms and shoulders. Driven back, Kilkenny swayed like a tree in a high wind, fighting desperately to stave off the attack.

There was a taste of blood in his mouth, and he felt his lungs gasping for breath. Every gasp was a tearing pain.

Had he a broken rib? It felt like he had.

Brockman closed in, sensing some weakness, and threw a left that might have ended the fight, had it landed. But Kilkenny went under it, butting the larger man in the chest. Missing a left, he split Cain's face with his elbow, turning his head half-around.

Despite the fierceness of the fighting, Kilkenny was not badly hurt. Many of the bigger man's blows had been wasted on his arms or shoulders. One of his eyes had a bad cut, and he knew by the feel that his jaw was swollen. But mainly he was fighting to stave off the big man's attacks, while trying to slow him down and sap his strength with body punches. But now he was growing desperate.

His hardest punches seemed to have no effect on Cain Brockman. The big man's face was bleeding from several cuts. Undoubtedly his nose was broken, and his lips were badly battered, but he now seemed to have gotten his second wind, and to be no less strong than when he threw his first punch.

Kilkenny realized that one of his eyes was rapidly swelling shut. His breath was coming in tearing gasps.

Brockman bored in, swinging. Kilkenny pushed the left outward and stepped in with a hard left uppercut to the wind that stopped Brockman in his tracks. But the big man bowed his head and moved in.

Dropping an open palm to Brockman's skull as the man pushed forward, he shoved him off-balance, then as his hands went wide to gain balance, Kilkenny stabbed a left to the cut eye.

Cain swung a kick for Kilkenny's kneecap. Kilkenny drove at him and hit Brockman at the knees. Both went down to the floor, Brockman's head hitting hard as he landed. Dazed, Brockman started up, then lunged in a long dive at Kilkenny, who promptly stepped back, then brought a knee up to Brockman's face.

Brockman went back down to his hands and knees on the floor, his face a bloody mask. He was still trying to get up. Kilkenny was sick of the fight, and sick of the beating he was now giving the big man.

As Brockman struggled up, Kilkenny feinted, then hit him in the solar plexus. Cain went down, gasping, struggling to get up but unable to.

Kilkenny stepped back. "It's enough. You're a tough man, Brockman, but I've other business."

Weaving, Kilkenny walked to the bar and braced himself with both hands, which were battered and swollen from punching. He stood there, panting heavily.

Rusty came up beside him. "Kilkenny, call it off! You're in no shape for that raid now! You're certainly in no condition to tackle Royal Barnes."

"To hell with it!" Kilkenny said. "You do your part, I'll do mine."

Walking back to the washbasin he spilled water from the pitcher and bathed his cut face and his bruised and swollen hands. Turning to Gates, who had followed him, he said, "I'll need some hot water and some salts . . . Epsom salts."

"Got a-plenty of it at the store," Frame said. "I'll get it."

Lance let his hands soak and gingerly bathed the caked blood from around the cuts. Frame returned not only with the salts but with a fresh shirt as well. "You'll need this," he said. "Consider it a gift. What a scrap! Man, I've seen a few, but—"

"He was tough," Kilkenny agreed. "I never saw a man take so much and keep coming back."

Joe Frame grunted. "Hell, man, you did pretty well yourself!"

The bartender brought hot water, and dumping the Epsom salts into it, Lance continued to soak his hands. There was nothing better for taking the stiffness and soreness from muscles or bruises, but it was his hands that worried Lance most. Those hands must handle the guns against Royal Barnes.

Although one eye was badly swollen, he could still see through the slit.

He had no choice but to go, for he was sure the others would never ride without him. None of them knew the lay of the land as well as he did, and there was none among them capable of facing Barnes alone.

"Better get something to eat," he suggested to Webb Steele. "We'll ride in one hour."

"Will you be all right?"

"I'll be ready."

Kilkenny was far from sure of that, for his hands had swollen from the battering, and he had no idea how quick or accurate he would be with a gun. Yet the salts and hot water had helped. He worked his fingers, gently rubbed his hands.

Royal Barnes . . . somehow Kilkenny had always known the time would come.

But he also had to think of Nita . . . She must not be hurt. She must not be endangered.

Polti was dead, and Abel Brockman was dead. Cain was not dead but he was out of it for awhile.

Who would be next?

CHAPTER XVIII

On Buck, Lance Kilkenny rode for Apple Canyon. He was dead-tired, his muscles felt heavy and weary. Yet he knew that the outdoor life he lived, with the simple food, had given him the stamina he would need to recover his strength.

Behind him, in a tight cavalcade, rode the men of the Lord and Steele ranches with a few extras from Botalla and the country around.

Gates rode up beside him. "You had quite a scrap," he said. "I never knew you were a fist-fighter, too."

"I've boxed some. And I worked some in the lumberwoods as a youngster."

"You never did say where you were from," Gates suggested.

Kilkenny smiled. "No, I never did."

Rusty waited for awhile but nothing further was offered. Then he said, "Facing Barnes with hands like that may be suicide."

"Nevertheless, I have to do it. And my hands aren't as bad as they look. It isn't going to be speed that will win, not in this fight. We'll both catch lead, and the winner will be the one who can take the most and still keep coming.

"The way I see it, we'll be spotted before we ever get there. They'll be holed up around the buildings. The bunkhouse, the livery stable and the blacksmith shop all look like they were built to stand a siege."

"That was the idea," Rusty said. "They're built of heavy logs or stone, and built solid. Bill Sadler's place, on the same side as the Border Bar, is adobe, and its walls are three feet thick, with windows set to cover the trail into town. It'll be no picnic, believe me!"

"I know," Kilkenny rubbed Buck's neck thoughtfully. "We've got to figure that one out, but I'll not be there for much of it. I'll be going up to the house, up there on the cliff."

"Alone?" Gates was incredulous. "Man, you're asking for it. He'll be forted up with a dozen others, waiting for you."

"I doubt it. I doubt if he ever lets more than one man stay up there with him. Royal Barnes, as I understand him, isn't a trusting soul. My idea is to come down from the cliffs above the house."

"You're crazy!" Gates protested. "They're sheer rock! You'd need a rope and a lot of luck. And even then he'd see you and nail you before you ever got down!"

"Maybe. I've got the rope, and maybe the luck. Anyway, I'll come down behind him where he won't be expecting trouble, and I'll come while you boys are keeping them busy down below. Now listen . . . this is the way I see it—"

As Webb, Frame and Rusty listened, Kilkenny outlined a plan of attack.

"It might work," Steele said.

Kilkenny had no illusions about the task they had set for themselves. With the plan he had conceived, the details carefully worked out during the days that had passed, he believed the fort houses of Apple Canyon might be taken.

It meant a struggle, and there would be loss of life. This riding column would lose some of its numbers before it returned, and there would surely be bloody fighting before the job was completed.

Where was Steve Lord? Had Steve taken the bait and gone to the hidden cabin in the box canyon? It would be a place to look.

Kilkenny shrank from the task, even the idea, and only the knowledge that others would die if he didn't act would even permit him to consider it. Luckily,

the canyon was only a short distance from the route
the cavalcade must follow.

There had been no diary left by Des King. That
diary had existed only in Kilkenny's imagination, and
had been bait he had dropped to lure the killer.

Of course, he would have learned the answer soon,
in any event, even if Chet Lord had not told him, for
the evidence had been accumulating slowly. He had
been suspicious of Steve Lord and waited only for a
chance to check Steve's guns against the shells he had
found.

What would Steve Lord do now? He was outlawed.
He knew that his father had exposed him, and he
must realize there was evidence enough to convict him
or to send him to an asylum for the insane. He would
be desperate. Would he try again to kill Kilkenny?
Or would he go on one last killing spree and shoot
everybody and everything in sight?

Kilkenny had a hunch that Steve would ride for Apple Canyon. Several times, Kilkenny recalled, he had
come upon Steve either on that trail or in the vicinity,
and at least once Steve had been rather sharp in his
inquiries as to what Kilkenny was doing there.

Was Steve interested in Nita Riordan?

He turned to Webb Steele. "You boys stay on the
trail to Apple Canyon. I'll turn off to that shack
where I let Steve think Des King had left a diary,
and when I find Steve, I'll come back."

He wheeled the buckskin and took off up a draw
into the steeper hills. He had been thinking of this
route as he rode along. Although he was not sure the
route would take him where he wished to go, he knew
he would find a way.

He emerged on to a small plain of bunch grass
dotted with clumps of oak. All the ridges were covered
with scrub oak. He paused among the trees to wipe the
sweat from his hatband and brow, then slid his Winchester from the scabbard and rode on.

He kept working his fingers. They were a little stiff,
but felt better than he had expected.

He struck a long unused path and followed it through
the trees. The trail wound upward, then left the trees

and topped out in a region of heaped-up boulders, where the trail wound with all the casualness of cow trails in a country where cows are in no hurry. Twice, rabbits leaped up and scurried away, but the buckskin's hoofs made no sound on the soft grass.

Kilkenny was cutting across a meadow when he saw the prints of a horse bisecting the trail he was making. In the tall grass of the meadow, the tracks were too indistinct to tell him anything about the horse, but on a hunch he turned the buckskin and followed.

Whoever the rider was, he was in a hurry, riding toward his objective in as straight a line as possible.

It had bad features, this trailing a man in country where he alone was native. Such a man would know of routes and places of concealment of which Kilkenny could know nothing. Such an advantage could mean the difference between life and death.

Scanning every open space before he crossed it, Kilkenny followed the trail with care. He knew only too well how little it required to conceal a man. A few inches of grass, clothing that blended with the surroundings, and immobility were the only essentials to remaining unseen.

Sunlight caught the highest ridges, and slowly the long shadows crept higher, and the light almost disappeared down the quiet canyons. Kilkenny, every sense alert for trouble, rode warily.

When the cabin was not far away, he dismounted and faded into the darkness under the shadowing trees, looking down through the narrow opening into the box canyon.

It was a squat, shapeless structure, built hurriedly by some wandering prospector or casual sheepherder long, long ago. In the years that had followed, the roof had sagged here and there, branches had been added and earth piled atop until the roof had become a mound now covered with grass.

It was an ancient, decrepit structure, its one window a black hole, its door too low for a tall man.

About it the grass was green, for there was a small stream nearby that flowed from the rocks near the cabin, crossed the box canyon diagonally and flowed back into a hole in the rock on the far side. In transit, it watered a small meadow.

Outside the cabin, under a lone apple tree, stood a saddled horse, his head hanging.

"There we are," Lance muttered. "Now to get close!"

Leaving the buckskin hidden, he crossed a narrow stretch in a crouching run to the nearest boulder, then on to a clump of brush and trees. Crouching there, he watched the cabin.

There should have been a light in there by now, but there was none. It should take no time to search the cabin, but it would be too dark in there to see much. He hesitated, scanning the rocks and the cliffs. He saw nothing.

The saddled horse stood, head low, waiting wearily. A breeze stirred the leaves of some cottonwoods near the stream. They whispered softly to one another in the evening air. Pulling his sombrero lower, Kilkenny moved with the whispering leaves to cover the rustle of his movement, slipping into the bottleneck entrance of the canyon.

There was no shot, no sound. The horse moved a little, began idly cropping grass, yet he acted as if he had been doing that for some time, and was no longer hungry. Suddenly Kilkenny had a feeling that the cabin was empty.

There was no reason to delay. He would go over to it.

He stepped out, rifle ready, and walked swiftly and silently across the grass to the cabin.

The blackness gave off no sound. Despite himself, he was suddenly uneasy. It was too still, and there was something almost unearthly about the squat cabin and the lost, lonely canyon.

He shifted his rifle to his left hand and drew a six-gun, which was better for close quarters.

Then he looked in.

The inside was black, yet between himself and the hole that passed for a window he could see the vague outline of the head of a sleeping man . . . at least a man seated, with his head bowed forward on his chest.

"All right," he spoke clearly, if not loudly. "You can get up and come out!"

There was neither sound nor movement. Kilkenny stepped inside, gun ready. And still there was no movement.

Taking a chance, he struck a match.

The man was dead.

He glimpsed a stump of candle on the table, and lit it.

The man was a stranger, a middle-aged man and, by his looks, a cowhand. He had been shot in the right temple by someone who had fired from the window. The room had been thoroughly ransacked.

Kilkenny went out quickly. There was nothing to do now but return. The dead man's horse was only ground-hitched and there was plenty of grass and water.

Buck returned to the trail with quickened step, as if aware that the end was near. Kilkenny lounged in the saddle. Steve Lord would be riding hard now, heading for Apple Canyon. He would know nothing of their projected attack.

Weary from the long ride and the fight with Cain Brockman, Kilkenny sagged in the saddle, and the yellow horse ambled along the trail, taking its own gait, drifting through the shadows like a ghost horse on a ghost trail.

There was a faint light in the sky, the barest hint of daybreak in the sky when Kilkenny at last rode up to join the posse.

They were gathered in a shallow valley about two miles from the canyon. Dismounted, aside from a few guards, they stood around a couple of small fires. Kilkenny could smell coffee, and frying bacon.

He swung down and walked to the fire, his boots sinking in the soft sand of the wash. Firelight brought out highlights and shadows on the hard, unshaven faces of the men.

Webb Steele, squatted by the fire, his big body looming as huge as a grizzly's, looked up. "Find Steve?"

"No . . . But he killed another man . . . a stranger." Briefly, he explained what he had found at the cabin.

"Steve rode on. He's probably down there at the town."

"You think he worked with this gang? Against his own pa?"

"Could be. I think he knows Barnes, although that's only a guess. I think they cooked up some kind of a deal, and I think Steve has a leaning toward Nita Riordan. That may be why he came here."

Rusty made no comment. The tough redhead looked pale. He had been in no shape for the hard ride, but would not be left behind. Wounded or not, he was worth two ordinary men.

Not two like Webb Steele, however. Or Old Joe Frame. Either would do to ride the river with. They might be bullheaded, and they might argue and talk a lot, but they were men who believed in doing the right thing, and men who would fight in order to do it.

Glancing around at the others, Kilkenny saw what he expected. Most of them were tough, rough and ready cowhands who rode for the brand. All of them had been through such fights before, and many another season of trouble. Like a stampede, a river-swimming or a hailstorm, they took it in stride.

Kilkenny accepted gratefully the cup of hot, black coffee that was put in his hand. Sipping it was pure delight after the long, hard ride.

"We'd better mount up," he said. "The light's coming on."

Webb Steele looked around at his men. "You all know what this is about. They ain't about to back up and quit and we aren't planning on any prisoners. If a man cuts and runs, let him go if he drops his shootin' iron. If he doesn't, he may be going to a better position, so drop him.

"Those who do throw down their guns, take 'em prisoner. We'll try 'em all an' hang the guilty ones, but there'll be mighty few who are innocent in Apple Canyon."

"One thing," Kilkenny interrupted. "Leave Nita Riordan, her Border Bar and her house alone."

He was not at all sure how the men would accept that, but he didn't care. He saw tacit approval in

Rusty's eyes. Steele and Frame nodded agreement. Then his eyes encountered the eyes in a tall, lean, cadaverous face. The man chewed silently a moment, staring at Kilkenny.

"I reckon," he said harshly, "that if we clear the bad 'uns out of Apple, we better clear 'em all out. Me, I ain't stoppin' for no woman. Nor that halfbreed man of her'n, either!"

Steele's fingers closed in a fist and there was a sudden tension in the crowd. Was there to be a split now? At such a time?

Kilkenny smiled. "No reason for any trouble, but she gave me a tip once that helped. I believe she's friendly to us and I believe she's innocent of any wrongdoing."

The man with the cold eyes looked right back at him. "I aim to clear her out of here, as well as the others. I aim to burn that place down over her head."

There was cruelty in the man's face and a harshness that seemed to spring from some inner source of malice and hatred. He wore a gun tied down and had a carbine in the hollow of his arm. Several others moved closer to him, an odd similarity in their faces.

"There'll be time to settle that," Kilkenny said quietly, "when we get there. But you'd better change your mind, my friend. If you don't, you're going to have to kill me right along with her."

"She's a scarlet woman," the man said viciously, "and dyin's too good for her kind! I'm a-gettin' her, an' you stay clear!"

"Time's a-wastin'," Steele interrupted. "Let's ride!"

In the saddle, Kilkenny rode beside Steele. "Who is that hombre?" he demanded.

"Name of Calkins, Lem Calkins. Hails from West Virginia, and he's a feuder. I've met some good folks from there, but Calkins is a mean, hard man.

"Did you see those who grouped around him? He's got three brothers and five sons. You touch one of them and you've got to fight them all!"

They rode over the rise and into Apple Canyon, and Kilkenny wheeled his horse and raced toward the cliff. Instantly a shot rang out, and he turned the buckskin on a dime and charged into the street of the town.

More shots sounded, and a man drawing water at a well dropped the bucket and grabbed for his gun. Kilkenny snapped a shot and the man staggered, grabbing at his arm. His gun lay in the dust. A shot whipped past Kilkenny, another ricocheted off his pommel but missed him and he raced his horse between Nita's house and the Border Bar and dropped from the saddle.

He went up the back steps in two jumps and sprang through the door. Firing had broken out in front, but Kilkenny's sudden attack from the rear was a complete surprise. He snapped a shot at a lean redhead, and the man went down, grabbing at his chest with both hands.

The bartender reached for the sawed-off shotgun, and Kilkenny took him out with a shot from his left-hand gun.

Jaime Brigo sat tilted back in a chair at the end of the room. He had neither moved nor reached for a gun.

Kilkenny reloaded his pistols. "Brigo, there are some men who would harm the senorita. Lem Calkins and his brothers. They would burn this place and kill her. You savvy?"

"*Sí*, senor."

"I must go up the cliff. You must watch over the senorita. I will be back when I can."

Jaime Brigo got up. He towered above Kilkenny, and he smiled.

"Of course, senor. I know Senor Calkins well. He is a man who thinks himself good, but he is cruel. He is also a dangerous man."

"If necessary," said Kilkenny, "take the senorita away, Brigo. I shall be back when I have seen the man on the cliff."

The firing was increasing in intensity.

"Have you seen Steve Lord?" Kilkenny asked.

"*Sí*. He went before you to the cliff. The senorita would not see him and he was very angry. He said he would return soon, and she would see him then."

Kilkenny stood alone in the middle of the room for

a moment. He thought about the place on the hill, and the odds. He was a man who never blinded himself to the realities, yet he had faith.

Now he must go . . . The time had come.

CHAPTER XIX

Kilkenny studied the street outside. The bulk of the outlaws seemed to have holed up in the livery stable and they were putting up a hot fire. Others had taken positions behind a pile of stones beyond the street and still others in the bunkhouse. There was no way to estimate their numbers.

Some of the attacking party had closed in, getting into positions from which they could fire into the face of the building, covering its windows and door. For the time being, it appeared to be a stalemate.

Walking to the back door of the saloon, Kilkenny slipped out into the yard and walked over to Buck. Concealed by the saloon building, he was out of the line of fire.

Suddenly Lance heard a low call. Glancing over, he saw Nita standing under the roses. Hesitating only for a quick look around, he crossed to her, leading the horse. For a moment he was exposed, but he got by unseen.

He told her of Lem Calkins. She nodded. "I expected that. He hates me."

"Why?"

"Oh, because I'm a woman, I guess. He came here once and had to be sent away. He seemed to believe I was a somewhat different person than I am."

"I see."

"You're going to the cliff?" Her eyes were wide and dark.

"Yes."

"Be very careful. There are traps up there. Spring guns, and other things."

"I shall be careful."

He swung to the saddle and loped the buckskin away, keeping the buildings between him and the firing.

When he had cleared Nita's house, a bullet winged past him from the stonepile, but he brought the horse in behind a hummock of sand and let him run. From now on, he must work with speed and care.

Skirting the rocks, he rode Buck upstream through the foot-deep water for half a mile, then went up the bank and rode a weaving trail through the willows. He scrambled up a steep draw to a plateau. Using a towering thumb-like butte for a marker he worked his way higher until he was sure he was behind the cliff house and well above it. At a secluded place among the rocks, where there was considerable grass, he slipped the reins over Buck's head and trailed them. "Take care of yourself, Buck. I've got things to do."

Leaving his rifle in its scabbard, Kilkenny left the horse and worked his way down through a maze of rocks toward the cliff edge.

The view was splendid. Far below he could see the scattered houses of Apple Canyon, and from here he could see occasional puffs of smoke. The sounds of gunshots seemed farther away than they were.

His own attacking party had fanned out in a long skirmish line across the pass and down toward the town. They were moving according to plan, shrewdly and carefully, never exposing themselves.

Kilkenny had planned it himself. He was sure from what he had learned that the well across from Nita's house was the only source of water. The one bucket was empty. He knew because it lay in plain sight near the well—alongside it the gun the man had dropped when Kilkenny had shot him.

There were a lot of men defending Apple Canyon, and it was going to be a long, hot day. If they could be pinned down, kept from getting water, and if he could eliminate Royal Barnes, there was a chance of complete surrender on the part of the outlaws.

He believed he could persuade Steele and Frame to let them go if they surrendered as a body and agreed to leave the country. His wish was to prevent any losses among their own men while breaking up the Barnes gang.

Suddenly, even as he watched, a man dashed from the rear of the bunkhouse toward the well and the fallen bucket. He was halfway to the well before a gun spoke, and Kilkenny would have sworn it was Mort Davis' old buffalo gun that did the job. Just from the sound.

The runner pitched forward on his head and fell face down on the hard-packed earth near the well. That would hold them for awhile. Nobody wanted to die that way. By now they were doing a lot of thinking, for every man jack of them had a sense of the time and the sun.

There appeared to be at least six hundred feet to the floor of the valley from where Kilkenny stood. Recalling his calculations, he believed it would be about fifty feet down to the cliff house and the window he had selected.

Undoubtedly there was an exit somewhere among the boulders and crags not far from his horse, but there was no time to look for it now.

He had taken his rope from his saddle and now he made it fast around the trunk of a gnarled old cedar, then he stepped off the cliff, easing himself down. His hands seemed to be working well.

He was halfway down when the first shot came, and it came from the livery stable. The bullet spat rock fragments into his face that stung like blown needles, but instantly his own crowd opened up a strong covering fire. He glanced down, trying to locate the window. It was a bit to his right.

Careful to make no sound, he lowered himself still more.

He was almost at the window.

Another shot clipped the rock near him. Whoever

was shooting was taking hasty shots without proper aim, or he wouldn't have missed. Kilkenny was thanking his stars that the men behind the stone pile had not seen him when a shot cut through his sleeve and stung his arm.

Involuntarily, he jerked and almost lost his hold. Just as bullets began to spatter around him, his feet found a toehold on the windowsill. The window was open and he dropped inside.

Instantly, he slipped out of the line with the window and froze. Standing very still, he listened.

The room was a small bedroom, with Indian blankets spread on the bed, and a crude table and chair.

He rested a hand on the latch of a door and lifted it slowly.

"Come in, Kilkenny! Come right on in!"

Kilkenny pushed the door open with his left hand and stepped into the room, every sense alert and poised for a fast draw, if need be.

It was a neat and sun-filled room. At a table alone sat a man in a white, open-necked shirt, a broad leather belt and gray trousers tucked into cowhide boots. He also wore two guns.

He was clean-shaven except for a neatly trimmed mustache, and he wore a black silk scarf around his neck.

It was Victor Bonham.

"So?" Kilkenny said, smiling. "I might have suspected."

"Of course. Bonham or Barnes, whichever you prefer. Most people call me Royal Barnes."

"I've heard of you."

"And I, of you."

Barnes's lips smiled, but there was no smile in his eyes. "You've been making trouble for me, again."

"Again?" Kilkenny lifted an eyebrow.

"Yes . . . You killed the Webers. A bungling lot, the Webers, but they are kinfolk, and some of my relatives think because you killed them that I must kill you. It's probably as good a reason as any."

"It could be a reason . . . Do you need one?"

"No."

Barnes glanced at his nails. "You were asking to die, coming in that way."

"Safer than the other way," Kilkenny said, gently.

"So? Somebody talked, did they? Well, it is time I got new men, anyway. But you're a fool, Kilkenny. This little affair is not going to stop me, or even slow me down. I'll have to recruit a new bunch of men, but you will lose men, too. Today some of the best men in the Live Oak country will die—and there will be just that many I will no longer have to plan for.

"Next time it will be much easier, and I intend to reorganize, recruit the men I need and come back. I'd have succeeded this time but for you.

"Steele will fight but, if he isn't killed today, I will see him dead before the week is out. That goes for your friend Rusty Gates and for Joe Frame, as well. Gates isn't dangerous alone, but he might find another man like you with whom to work.

"Usually there are only a few men in any community who are dangerous to efforts like mine. Eliminate them, and the rest are afraid to step out of the crowd."

The tempo of the firing had increased. Without looking, Kilkenny knew his men were in and out among the buildings now. Yet Barnes did not allow his eyes to shift for one instant. He was wary as a crouched tiger. In the quiet, well-ordered room, he seemed aloof from all down below. He seemed like someone from another world, another lifetime. Only his eyes showed what was in him.

"Have you seen Steve Lord?"

"Lord?" Barnes' eyes seemed to change a little. "He never comes here."

"He worked with you."

Barnes shrugged. "Of course. One has to use the tools at hand, so I held out Nita as bait. Nita and power. I promised him the Steele ranch. He is a fool."

"Do you know how many men he's killed?"

"Steve?" Barnes was incredulous. "He's yellow. He wouldn't kill anybody."

Kilkenny smiled, shaking his head. "Barnes," he said, "that's just shows how wrong you can be. Steve is crazy. There's something inside him that's driving him to kill, and he'll never stop now until somebody kills him. He killed Des King. He killed Sam Carter and he's killed a half-dozen others. Now he's gunning for you!"

Royal Barnes was annoyed. "Don't be foolish! He isn't dry behind the ears yet! He'd never kill anyone!"

Nonetheless, Kilkenny could see that the idea that he could make such a mistake had annoyed and irritated him.

Royal Barnes got up suddenly. "Somebody is on the trail now!"

"That could be Steve," Kilkenny replied, suddenly aware that Barnes was awaiting some sound, some signal. If there was a spring gun on the main trail, it would stop Steve in his tracks.

Somewhere he could hear water dripping—slowly, methodically, as if counting off the seconds. Royal Barnes put his hand to a deck of cards on the table and idly riffled them. The spattering sound of the cards was loud in the room.

Again there was the heavy boom of the buffalo gun. That must be Mort Davis again. Somebody had probably tried to get water.

Gravel rattled on the trail, and Kilkenny saw the skin tighten around Barnes's eyes.

Then, in almost complete silence, the heavy *boom* of a shotgun in a confined space!

Royal Barnes went for his gun. He had been half facing Kilkenny. As he drew he shoved the table toward him.

The floor was slippery and the table, prepared for just such a move, shot toward Kilkenny across the hardwood floor.

"But Barnes had not calculated Kilkenny's incredibly quick reaction. The same leap that took him from behind the table, enabled the bullet to miss.

Kilkenny palmed his gun and fired twice, so rapidly the shots blended into one sound. Through the smoke he could see Royal Barnes's eyes, blazing with some strange light, his lips drawn in a snarl of fury.

Then all sight and all other sound was lost in the

thunderous roar of heavy guns in the confined space.

He was shooting. He was hit. He felt his back smashed against the wall, and through the smoke he could see the stab of crimson flame.

His own guns were firing. He stepped left, then right. Barnes sprang backward through a doorway, and Kilkenny paused, thumbing cartridges into his guns.

He was breathing hoarsely, and the room was filled with the acrid smoke of black powder. He crossed the room and went through the door, low and fast. A bullet smashed into the doorjamb near his face. Another tugged at his sleeve with invisible fingers.

He stepped over, saw Barnes, and fired on the instant. Flame blossomed from Barnes's guns and Kilkenny felt his knees give way. He went down. Royal Barnes was backing away, his eyes wide and staring, his shirt-front bathed in blood.

Pulling himself erect with his left hand, Kilkenny fired again. He started to shoot once more but Barnes was gone.

Stumbling on into the next room, he stared about him. He was sick and faint, weaving on his feet, and blood was running into his eyes.

The room was empty. A gun fired behind him and he turned in a stumbling circle and saw a shadow weaving before him through the gunsmoke. Kilkenny opened up with both guns, and then he fell. He went down hard.

He must have blacked out briefly, an instant only, but when his senses returned the room was acrid with the smell of powder smoke. He got his knees under him, retrieved his left-hand gun and, using the fingers of that hand, helped himself erect before resuming a full grip on the pistol.

All sense of time and space was gone. He had but one thought. Royal Barnes was here, and Royal Barnes must die.

Then he saw him, propped against the opposite wall. A bullet had gone through one cheek, entering below the nose and coming out under the ear. Blood was flowing from the wound. Barnes was cursing through bloody, foam-flecked lips, cursing in a low, ugly-monotone.

"You got me, damn you! But I'm taking you with me!"

His gun swung up. Kilkenny's guns seemed to fire of their own volition. Barnes's body winced and jerked with the impact, then he lunged off the wall, his guns roaring. He was wild, insane, and desperate, but his guns no longer fired with the will of the man behind them. They simply fired, and the shots went wild.

He was toe-to-toe with Kilkenny when Kilkenny finished with four shots, two from each gun, at three-foot range. Then Barnes fell, tumbling across Kilkenny's feet and almost knocking him down.

For what seemed an eternity, Kilkenny stood erect, his guns dangling and empty. He stared blankly at the dead man at his feet, then at the weird pattern of the Navajo rug across the room. He could hear the hoarse rasp of his own breathing. He could feel the warm blood on his face. He could feel weakness mounting within him.

Suddenly, he heard a sound. He had dropped one of his guns. He stared down at it, uncomprehendingly. Abruptly, he seemed to have let go of everything and he fell, tumbling across Barnes's body to the floor. He felt warm sunlight on his face, then nothing more.

A long time later he felt hands touching him, felt his own hand reaching for his gun. A big man loomed over him. He was trying to lift his gun when a woman's voice spoke softly, and something in him listened. He let go of the gun.

He seemed to feel water on his face, and then pain throbbing inside him like a thing alive, tearing at his vitals. Then he went away again into a dark world where there was no thought or memory or pain.

When finally he again became conscious he was lying on a bed in a sunlit room. Outside there were flowers and he could hear a bird singing. There was a flash of red as a cardinal flirted past the window.

It was a woman's room, a quiet room, A curtain stirred in a cool breeze. He was lying there, barely awake, when Nita came in.

"So you're awake at last!" Her relief was obvious. "We were about to believe you'd never come out of it."

"What happened?" he mumbled.

"You were badly shot up. Six times in all, but only one of them really serious."

"Barnes?"

"He's dead. He was almost shot to pieces."

Kilkenny was quiet then. He closed his eyes and lay without moving for what seemed a long time. In all his experience he had never known a man with such vitality as Royal Barnes. Kilkenny rarely missed, and even in the wild and hectic battle in the cliff house he had known his shots were scoring. Yet Barnes had kept coming, had kept shooting.

He opened his eyes again. Only a moment had passed, because Nita was still standing there.

"Steve Lord?" he asked.

"He was killed by a spring gun, trying to get at Barnes. It was a double-barrelled shotgun loaded with soft lead pellets. He must have died instantly."

"The outlaws?"

"Wiped out. A few escaped during the last minutes, but not many. Webb Steele was wounded but not too badly. He's been up and around for several days."

"Several days? How long have I been here?"

"You were badly hurt, Lance. The fight was two weeks ago."

Kilkenny lay quiet for awhile, absorbing that. Then he remembered.

"Lem Calkins?"

"He was killed, he and two of his family. Jaime did it. Then Steele told the others either to leave us alone or fight them all, and they backed down."

The two weeks more that Kilkenny spent in bed drifted slowly by, but toward the end, as his strength returned, he became restless and worried.

He remained in Nita's room, cared for by her,

visited almost daily by Rusty, Tana and Webb Steele.
Joe Frame dropped by from time to time, as did some
of the others.

Lee Hall came by with Mort Davis, but Kilkenny
kept thinking of the buckskin and the long, lonely
trails.

Then one morning he got up early and went to the
corral. Rusty and Tana had come in the night before
and he saw their horses in the corral with Buck. He
saddled up and led the yellow horse outside.

The sun was just coming up and the morning air
was cool and soft. He could smell the sagebrush and
the mesquite. He felt restless and strange. Instinctively he knew that he faced a crisis more severe than any
brought on by his recent gun battle. Here, his life
could change, but would it be for the best?

"I don't know, Buck," he said, caressing the yellow
horse, "maybe we'd better take a ride and think it
over. Out in the hills with the wind in my face I can
think better."

He turned at the sound of a footstep and saw Nita
standing behind him. She looked fresh and lovely in a
print dress, and her eyes were gentle as they met his.

Kilkenny looked away quickly, cursing inwardly at
his weakness.

"Are you going, Kilkenny?" she asked.

"I reckon I am, Nita. Out there in the hills I can
think a sight clearer. I got a few things to figure out."

"Kilkenny," Nita asked suddenly, "why do you not
always talk like an educated man?"

She paused. "Tana told me you once dropped a
picture of your mother, and there was an inscription on
it—something about it being sent to you in college."

"I can speak like an educated man, Nita, but a lot
of us out here have sort of taken on the vernacular of
the country." He hesitated, then added, "I'd better be
riding now."

There were tears in her eyes but she lifted her head
and smiled at him.

"Of course, Kilkenny. Go, and if you decide you
wish to come back . . . don't hesitate. And Buck," she

turned quickly to the yellow horse, "if he starts back you bring him very fast, do you hear?"

For an instant Kilkenny hesitated again, then he swung into the saddle.

The buckskin wheeled and they went out of Apple Canyon at a brisk trot. Once he looked back and Nita was standing as he had left her. She lifted her hand and waved.

He waved in return, then faced away to the west. The wind came over the plains, fresh with morning, and he lifted his eyes, scanning the horizon. The buckskin's ears were forward, and he was quickening his pace, eager to move into the distance.

"You 'an me, Buck," Kilkenny said, "we just ain't civilized. We're wild, and we belong to the far, open country where the wind blows and a man's eyes narrow down to distance."

Kilkenny glanced back. There was no sign of Apple Canyon now, there was only the horizon . . . it might have been any horizon.

He lifted his voice and sang.

> *I have a word to speak, boys, only*
> *one to say,*
> *Don't never be no cow-thief,*
> *don't never ride no stray.*
> *Be careful of your rope, boys,*
> *and keep it on the tree,*
> *But suit yourself about it,*
> *for it's nothing at all to me!*

He sang softly, and the hoofs of the buckskin kept time to the singing, and Lance could feel the air on his face. A long way ahead the trail curved into the mountains.

ABOUT THE AUTHOR

Louis L'Amour, born Louis Dearborn L'Amour, is of French-Irish descent. Although Mr. L'Amour claims his writing began as a "spur-of-the-moment thing," prompted by friends who relished his verbal tales of the West, he comes by his talent honestly. A frontiersman by heritage (his grandfather was scalped by the Sioux), and a universal man by experience, Louis L'Amour lives the life of his fictional heroes. Since leaving his native Jamestown, North Dakota, at the age of fifteen, he's been a longshoreman, lumberjack, elephant handler, hay shocker, flume builder, fruit picker, and an officer on tank destroyers during World War II. And he's written four hundred short stories and over fifty books (including a volume of poetry).

Mr. L'Amour has lectured widely, traveled the West thoroughly, studied archaeology, compiled biographies of over one thousand Western gunfighters, and read prodigiously (his library holds more than two thousand volumes). And he's watched thirty-one of his westerns as movies. He's circled the world on a freighter, mined in the West, sailed a dhow on the Red Sea, been shipwrecked in the West Indies, stranded in the Mojave Desert. He's won fifty-one of fifty-nine fights as a professional boxer and pinch-hit for Dorothy Kilgallen when she was on vacation from her column. Since 1816, thirty-three members of his family have been writers. And, he says, "I could sit in the middle of Sunset Boulevard and write with my typewriter on my knees; temperamental I am not."

Mr. L'Amour is re-creating an 1865 Western town, christened Shalako, where the borders of Utah, Arizona, New Mexico, and Colorado meet. Historically authentic from whistle to well, it will be a live, operating town, as well as a movie location and tourist attraction.

Mr. L'Amour now lives in Los Angeles with his wife Kathy, who helps with the enormous amount of research he does for his books. Soon, Mr. L'Amour hopes, the children (Beau and Angelique) will be helping too.